Children for Sale

The Complete Series

Jasper Joshua West

Copyright © 2020 Jasper Joshua West

All rights reserved.

ISBN: 9798647202888

Table of Contents

Get your FREE book!................................4

Taken 7

Far from Home 123

Second Hand 247

Twelve Days of Trauma (sample)........ 355

More by JJ West 377

Get your FREE book!........................... 379

CHILDREN FOR SALE

Get your FREE book!

Click, tap or type in bookHip.com/lkcwpk

Part One

Taken

Children For Sale: foren

Chapter One

JAMIE SQUINTED, running from his classroom, his eyes adjusting to the sunlight after hours indoors. Being released for recess was so liberating after sitting inside for lessons all morning. It was an unusually hot day in Massachusetts, and he could already feel sweat forming on his neck as he ran. He faintly heard young girls singing and giggling in the distance as he sprinted as fast as he could to the swings.

The swing set is a hot commodity during every recess— and if you are not one of the first kids to grab a swing, you're out of luck for the day. When Jamie finally reached the swings, he was disappointed to find that three kids had already claimed them for the duration of their break. He frowned and made his way over to his usual spot during recess.

When Jamie's parents first told him that he would be moving to a new school, he was excited. For weeks he had been fantasizing about how wonderful it was going to be, until he walked into the classroom and realized that he was not prepared at all. There was so much in the room that it was hard to take it all in; posters displaying 3D shapes and famous people, and stations set up all around the room. It was so much better than he could ever have imagined.

Snack time was way better than at his old school and he loved art class, but what Jamie was looking forward to the most, and was struggling with the most, was making new friends.

He got to the corner of the fence where he usually sat while waiting for a swing and he sat down. Leaning on the fence, though, he felt himself starting to fall. He caught himself and moved over, looking for the reason for having fallen only to discover that the fence had been cut. He felt a bee sting his neck and he moved to smack it off of him, but what he felt was not an insect. He tried to remove the object when the world went black and he fell to the ground.

Chapter Two

SHARON GILES SIGHED as her house phone rang, interrupting the folding of laundry. She answered the phone to hear a chatter of incoherence, followed by, "Hello, is this Mrs. Giles?" the familiar voice asked.

"Yes, speaking," Sharon replied, trying to place the voice.

"This is Mrs. Spalding at Jamie's school," she said. Mrs. Spalding was the principal. "I'm afraid there is an emergency and we need you to come right away."

Sharon was hyperventilating as tears pooled in her eyes "Is Jamie okay?" she shouted into the phone, fearing the worst.

"Jamie disappeared during recess and we cannot find him anywhere," the principal replied with pity in her voice. "We've already called the police."

Without another word, Sharon hung up the phone, grabbed her keys and jumped into her car. She quickly pulled out and headed for the school. As soon as she was capable of speaking coherently, she called her husband over the Bluetooth in her car, praying that he would answer while he was at work. Harry picked up on the third ring "Sharon? Is something wrong?" he answered in a worried tone. He knew she wouldn't bother him unless it was important.

Sharon frantically explained the phone call from the school and assured her husband that she was on her way to meet the police and the staff at the school.

"I'm leaving work right now," Harry said, brow furrowed. "I'll be at the school in 15 minutes."

Fifteen minutes later, Sharon arrived at the school at the same time as her husband and saw a multitude of police cars parked around the administration block. She met the lead detective, Detective Boyd, and answered his preliminary questions about her son. She felt the passing time weighing down on her as she answered as patiently as was possible: he is 9 years old; he was wearing a blue shirt and jeans; yes, he knows not to talk to strangers. She was still frantically checking the time slowly ticking by on her phone when Detective Boyd confirmed that Jamie had not been found within a 10-mile radius and that the investigation had been escalated.

Only minutes later a detective rushed towards the group, speaking the three golden words: "We found something."

Chapter Three

JAMIE slowly opened his eyes to find himself in an unfamiliar vehicle, and automatically assumed that he was dreaming. Looking to his left, he saw a sign informing him that he was leaving town. Looking up ahead he found that neither his mom nor his dad was driving. To his surprise, he did not see his mom's curly blonde hair or his dad's short black hair from his vantage point behind the driver's seat as he was accustomed to seeing.

Distracted by a slight movement at the far-right of the backseat, like someone trying to move as surreptitiously as possible, he focused his attention on the stranger looking at him in surprise. The woman with long, straight black hair, dull brown eyes, a nose piercing, and wearing a black dress was not anyone he recognized. He quickly made the assumption that it might well be a friend of one or both of his parents.

The woman spoke to the driver in a language unfamiliar to Jamie in an accent he could not pinpoint the origin of. This directed Jamie's attention back to the driver, who he was able to see more clearly now that he had turned to respond to the woman. He had a mean face, stringy black hair, and beady eyes that were constantly scanning his surroundings. When he opened his mouth to respond, chipped yellow teeth were visible, and his breath stank of alcohol and tobacco.

He replied in the same language, and the woman began undressing Jamie, confusing him and causing some apprehension for the first time.

At this point, Jamie realized that the drive wasn't a dream and that he was in real danger from these foreigners transporting him from the only town he'd ever known in his short life. He began to panic, saw the man and woman nodding simultaneously at one another with serious expressions, and he opened his mouth to scream. It was at this moment that he saw the woman produce a syringe filled with a clear liquid which she injected into the same place on his neck in which he had been poked on the playground.

He felt himself slip into darkness as he screamed.

Chapter Four

TO ANYONE LOOKING in from the outside, Harry seemed very calm about the situation with his son, considering detectives suspected more than just a child leaving of his own accord. Harry had always been the type to take care of others before himself, especially his wife. Harry was focused on making sure his wife was calm and trying to keep her from having a breakdown, despite his already having started. How could anyone dare to take his smart, wonderful, funny son from him? Yes, he had heard the statistics about deaths and missing children, and he had immediately googled the phenomenon which he had so unwittingly accepted as his current reality. There was no way anyone could ever willingly harm his kind, brave son. He was not even prepared to consider the worst implications of the situation.

Sharon and Harry couldn't have coaxed the information from the detective fast enough after he had admitted to having found something. Finding something is better than knowing nothing and continuing completely in the dark.

"They found Jamie's baseball cap in a trash can a few blocks away," said Detective Boyd. Sharon was visibly shaken, and Harry held her so tight that it seemed he was trying to hold them both together before they broke into little pieces. They had to stay strong for their son.

Harry made sure his wife would be fine standing on her own, and then asked to be taken immediately to the location where Jamie's hat was discovered. Two policemen were sifting through said trash can in search of further evidence and Harry was aware of officers going door-to-door looking for possible eyewitnesses.

He was permitted to stand in while the officers were questioning local residents, with instructions not to interfere, and that's what he did with every resident in the vicinity. He soon became discouraged with the same responses from so many. They were inside, watching television, in their bedrooms, eating. No one seemed to have been outside when Jamie's hat was discarded in the trash can. But how could that be so?

The officer Harry was shadowing was eventually done with interviewing. Harry took a break to calm down, still seething that witnesses had not been forthcoming in the area. The constant honking of car horns was making it decidedly difficult to concentrate, which was irritating him. It dawned on him that an inordinate traffic of vehicles seemed apparent and he considered his whereabouts and the reason behind the traffic on the road. Upon review, he realized that the road was a section of Interstate 195 and he formed a theory about what may have happened to his son. He demanded to be taken back to the school to speak with Detective Boyd immediately.

Chapter Five

"The office is calling for your dismissal, Kimberly," Mrs. Anderson announced before the whole class. Her voice snapped Kimberly out of a daydream, but she was just glad to be going home.

When Mrs. Anderson announced that she would be accompanying Kimberly, she became curious about the reason for a teacher's presence. Regardless of the odd condition that came with it, she was glad that she could go home and nap more comfortably.

As soon as the door closed to the classroom and they were alone in the hallway, the teacher's voice took on a sense of urgency, "It's an emergency, leave your things here and follow me." She proceeded to guide her towards the rear of the school and out the door which snapped shut behind her. Suddenly, Kimberly was all alone, searching out her mother's car so she could get herself home. She felt a sting on her neck and the world went dark.

Chapter Six

Back at the school, Harry jumped out of the police cruiser and demanded an audience with Detective Boyd. "Check the interstate!" Harry exclaimed when he regrouped with Boyd and his wife.

"We've alerted the State Police and they are looking for the vehicle on the interstate," said Boyd. "Now there is something that I need you to do to help. Could you get something that has Jamie's scent on in for the canine team?"

"Of course," Harry said, then turned to Sharon. "Will you be alright if I go home to get Jamie's favorite shirt, honey?"

"Yes, Harry, I'll be fine. Please just help them find our son as soon as they can."

Harry was escorted by the second-in-command, Officer Pearson, to their house. Harry walked in and went straight to Jamie's bedroom. Pearson followed and stood in the doorway.

"I know exactly what to use," Harry said, picking up Jamie's discarded pajamas from the floor. "These were his favorite pajamas, a gift from his uncle when they went to a Yankees game. They probably haven't been washed for a week or more," Harry said, holding up the navy-blue pajama top and pants covered in NY Yankees logos.

"That's perfect," Pearson said with a sad smile.

There was a silence between the two. Since when is finding your missing child's favorite pajamas something you get so excited about? Harry walked into his son's room again and looked around for a while, asking himself one question: If he ever saw his son again, what condition would he be in? The best-case scenario was that he was found happy and alive. Worst-case scenario was that he was found dead, murdered by someone who committed a senseless crime that would never be solved.

With his back to Pearson, Harry said, "I think some stranger has taken my son and is driving him God knows where on the interstate. I told your detective and he brushed it off. Are you going to brush it off?"

After a short pause, Pearson responded, "No, sir, I'm not. I have a daughter and I don't know what I would do in your position, probably go insane. I will do everything in my power to find your son."

Harry turned to Officer Pearson and they shared a moment as fathers, acknowledging the severity of the issue and how passionate they both were to solve the case and get Jamie safely home.

They smiled at each other and then got into the cruiser, to return to the school. Climbing out of the vehicle, Harry heard something through the radio that stopped him in his tracks. "...witness described a car that she saw a boy matching the given description getting into and leaving around the estimated time of the crime." Harry got out of the cruiser and said, "Find my boy," and Pearson nodded as he was pulling away to investigate the lead.

Chapter Seven

"We will keep you updated if-"

Boyd was cut off mid-sentence by an incoming phone call and raised a finger to indicate to Sharon that it was important. He listened intently, seemingly not wanting to miss a word of the call.

He quickly remarked, "We will be in touch very soon," and left, leaving Sharon with junior officers and the school principal. A minute or two later, Harry arrived and hugged his wife so tightly that it temporarily winded her.

"They might have an eyewitness who saw Jamie get into a car!" he told her. Looking into his eyes, his wife saw genuine excitement and the first real glimmer of hope since their son had gone missing.

Sharon hugged her husband as tightly as she possibly could and her eyes welled up with tears of joy as she whispered, "I love you, Harry. We're going to find him."

After the long, intimate hug, Harry grabbed Sharon's hand and led her out to his truck so they could contribute to the search for a car matching the witness's description. They met a team of officers at the SRTA terminal and offered to help in any way. They didn't need any help, so the two made their way to the next location, nearby. Once at the ferry pier, they separated to look around the parking lot.

After about ten minutes, just as Harry was about to suggest they give up and search somewhere else, he heard Sharon yell, "Over here!"

His heart started beating like a drum as he followed the sound of his wife's voice.

He rushed to her side and followed her line of vision to the inside of a car matching the unique description given. He saw what she was seeing: the shoes that Jamie was wearing that morning before he disappeared.

Chapter Eight

Jamie's eyes reluctantly opened to a sunny, blue sky. He saw the back of the strange, foreign woman from his dream. Or had it not been a dream? His thoughts were fuzzy, and the memories of the car ride were like a missing puzzle piece.

Becoming increasingly aware of his surroundings, he realized that he was gently rocking back and forth, making him slightly nauseous. He turned his head slightly and saw the sea and the fading shoreline. When he moved to stand up, the woman whipped her head around to face him and smiled.

"Shhh," she whispered, as his eyes became heavier, and he became all the more tired.

Chapter Nine

"Yes, this is Sharon and Harry Giles, calling from the State Pier Maritime Terminal. We found a car with our son's shoes inside, please come quick!"

Following Sharon's concise calls to both Detective Boyd and 911, the police showed up within 15 minutes and ran to the scene of their discovery.

They immediately gained access to the car and searched it thoroughly. When they were preparing to open the trunk, Harry and Sharon felt more fear than either had ever felt in their lives. What would they do if that trunk opened to reveal the corpse of their son staring back at them? What would their purpose in life be? If the trunk of that car exposed their son's lifeless corpse, they would both be very lost for a very long time; possibly forever.

The search of the backseat of the car revealed Jamie's shirt and the jeans he was wearing when he went missing. They also found the tags obviously hastily removed from the new clothes that Jamie would be wearing when they found him. Not if.

There had been some doubt at the start of the investigation that this was anything more than a child wandering off during school, but now it was crystal clear that it was a kidnapping.

Chapter Ten

"I can't believe they haven't found him yet. I thought we were so close. The longer it takes to find him, the less the chance we have of finding him alive," said Sharon with tears streaming down her face.

Harry replied, "We just have to keep faith that our boy will be found. We both know how smart and resourceful he is, Sharon." As he said this, he reached for her and wiped the tears from her face.

"I know, honey, it's just hard. Promise me that we will never stop looking for our baby," Sharon sobbed. Her voice was trembling but sure, as she put all of her frustrations, anger, and sadness into her request.

"I swear," Harry promised, his voice breaking on his words.

Even as they were having this conversation, both were experiencing doubt and fear. No matter how kind or smart Jamie was, the world is a harsh and cruel place, filled with monstrous, senselessly violent people. Even on the way to the police station to potentially get answers, it was hard to keep faith having had no communication with your missing child in more than a day.

When they arrived at the station, they were shocked to see FBI agents already there. Before they even had time to question this, Detective Boyd tracked them down and pulled them into a room to watch a surveillance video on a computer.

"We think that we have found your son boarding a boat with two adults this morning in this security footage. We would like you guys to take a second look," said the detective.

Harry's and Sharon's eyes grew wide and then Sharon let out a gasp. They were watching her son being half-dragged onto a boat by two strangers. Now that Sharon and Harry knew that their son was alive, they would stop at nothing to get him back.

Still recovering from the initial shock, they were approached by an FBI agent who said wearily, "Folks, your son is not the only child who has been taken."

Chapter Eleven

"I'm agent Harper, the lead investigator for an organized kidnapping ring that targets children. Unfortunately, Jamie has become a victim of this ring and he is one of many cases we are investigating.".

The look of disgust and shock on Sharon's face grew increasingly intense with every word that Agent Harper spoke. Sharon tightly gripped the arms of her chair with both hands, causing her knuckles to turn white while trying to process all the infuriating information she had just been told. Imagining several kids being drugged, kidnapped, and smuggled was somehow worse than seeing her child forcefully dragged onto the boat, drugged to the point that he was in and out of consciousness.

The FBI was not able to disclose every detail of the case, but they were able to explain the general overview of what they have gathered so far. There had been at least 20 recorded cases of kidnapping associated to this ring in the United States and Canada.

The culprits had always used the same method when initially abducting the children. They used tranquilizer darts and then drove them to the nearest location for docking boats. Their knowledge ends just there on the typical patterns of the abductors.

Harper shows them into the room used for investigating the case, where Harry is immediately drawn to a map indicating all the locations struck by the criminals.

"They are abducting children near the east coast and heading south with them."

"That is our understanding too, sir. What we can't seem to figure out is why," said Harper.

Chapter Twelve

Stacey Jacobs huffed in frustration as the alarm sounded on her phone, reminding her to fetch Kimberly. She tended to become so focused on her drawings that the hours flew by without her noticing. She slammed her sketchbook closed and grabbed her keys out of a bowl on her vanity, picked up her purse, and checked her hair in the mirror before she walked out the door.

She stepped out and locked the door behind her, immediately donning her sunglasses. It was such a sunny day, enough to be almost unbelievable. She got into her car and made her way to her daughter's school to collect her.

When she arrived, Kimberly wasn't in her normal spot on the bench, waiting to be picked up after the school day. After waiting for about 20 minutes, Stacey began to become impatient and anxious about her daughter's tardiness. She decided to check whether she had been waiting in the office for some reason. She parked her car in front of the office and rang the doorbell, which got the attention of the secretary, who recognized her immediately and buzzed her in.

"Good afternoon, Melissa, has Kimberly been in here for the last few minutes?" Stacey asked as she quickly scanned the room for her daughter.

"No, Stacey, I haven't seen her, but let me check on her attendance today," replied the secretary as she typed Kimberly's name into her computer to search the database.

A few minutes later, a look of confusion dawned on Melissa's face as she spoke, "It says here that she was absent for all her classes this afternoon."

"That's impossible, I didn't pick her up," Stacey said, starting to panic. "Call 911 and report her missing," she said and ran for her car. She entered the address to the police station into her GPS and made her way over there to file a report. She had already lost valuable hours to find her daughter without even knowing she was gone.

Chapter Thirteen

"Step out with your hands up," yelled the officer. They had finally managed to locate the boat from the surveillance tape showing Jamie being dragged onto a dock. A man was found on board, but he scurried down to the cabin as soon as they began closing in. They heard him moving around in the cabin down below and then there was silence.

The officer climbed down the ladder with his hand resting on his gun holster in case he needed to use it to defend himself from whatever he might encounter at the bottom. Once off the ladder, he quickly scanned the area and found the man face-down and motionless on the ground.

He slowly approached him, putting two fingers on his neck to check for a pulse. Thankfully, he was breathing, so they could question him when he regained consciousness.

They searched for the woman and Jamie, but there was no sign of them. The only indication that they were ever there was the surveillance tape showing them forcing Jamie onto the boat. He let out a huff, frustrated that they couldn't interrogate the man immediately, and called Detective Boyd to give him an update.

"We found the boat, sir. The man was on board, but the woman and the kid are gone."

Chapter Fourteen

Jamie's eyes slowly opened for the third time as the strange, foreign woman shook him awake. She yanked him to his feet and pulled him by the arm along the metal floor of a narrow hallway. He tried as best he could to keep up with her, tripping over his own feet and struggling to make out the hallway through blurred vision.

After what seemed like forever, he felt himself being lifted, but he was far too weak to fight back and simply went limp in her arms. He looked down at the metal floor, confused as to why they might have stopped. Then she reached down and pulled on a lever beyond Jamie's line of vision, and they began descending a flight of stairs. He was so dizzy, and it was so hard to keep his eyes open. What had she done to him?

His eyes flew open in alarm when she set him down roughly on yet another metal floor. He took the chance to scan his surroundings to the best of his abilities. He first noticed a toilet in front of him. Just before his pants were pulled down and she yelled at him, leaving him in no doubt as to what she wanted him to do. All his fear and confusion erupted at once as he peed into the tiny, metal toilet, the dark color of his pee indicating that he was dehydrated. After urinating in the toilet at her command, he was led to the far end of the small, dingy room.

Scanning the room further, he made out about 5 sets of triple bunk beds. They all had mats but no blankets or pillows, which was fine with him because the room was extremely warm, cramped, and suffocating. She took him by the hand and guided him over to the beds, and he had his first sense of relief since being abducted; he would finally be allowed a chance to rest for a while. No more moving or waking up in strange places; he was finally settling down, even if it was in a scary and unfamiliar metal room with no privacy.

She lifted him again and set him down on a lower bunk before turning around and walking out. He couldn't stop thinking about how hungry he was - when was the last time he had eaten? He yearned for his mother's homemade fresh-baked, gooey chocolate chip cookies and a tall glass of cold milk.

While the hunger was gnawing away at him, he was glad to finally have a comfortable place to sleep. He tossed and turned until he was comfortable enough to let their tranquilizing drugs carry him away into sleep again.

Chapter Fifteen

"I have something," a coast guard pilot broadcast over the radio. He looked down to see a man frantically paddling a boat carrying two more passengers which had stalled.

"Nearby units on the water, move in," instructed the lead officer of the coast guard branch of the search unit of the investigation. Once the paddler was surrounded, he put up his hands in surrender while a woman quickly forced a child into the cabin below the deck of the boat.

"Come out with your hands up, ma'am," the lead officer shouted as he pulled his gun from its holster and held it at the ready. She appeared on the ladder with a scowl on her face, and his team proceeded to handcuff them as soon as she was back on deck. Two officers went below, and one returned with the motionless body of a young girl in his arms.

"Does she have a pulse?" the lead investigator asked the officer.

"Yes sir, but it is very faint, she needs to get to a hospital immediately."

The lead investigator signaled to him and he gently took the girl into his arms.

"Get back to shore as soon as possible," he barked at the officer who was tasked with taking the boat back to be searched in order to gather forensic evidence.

Boyd got news of the girl being found and just as he ended the call his phone rang again.

"Sir, we tried to make another arrest at a private dock where a boat had been stolen came back," said the frantic officer on the phone. "The suspect fired on us and we returned fire, killing him."

When the boat was about 15 minutes from the closest docking station, all the officers' radios went off simultaneously, all sounding the same transmission, "We found more abandoned boats in the area that may be related to this case. Do you want us to bring them back as well, sir?"

A grave look dawned on the officer in charge's face as he said, "Bring them all."

They were almost back at the docks when an officer from the second boat found said, "I have some bad news, sir. Our third arrest and one of our only leads just passed away."

Chapter Sixteen

It was 5:30 and there were already 42 kidnappings committed by these criminals, including only the cases that were actually reported. There had been no progress in the Jamie Giles case, with seemingly constant new questions to be asked, but absolutely no answers to be found.

Hundreds of qualified professionals, soldiers, and civilians compiled of law enforcement, military, and volunteer groups had been searching for leads for hours. The latest update received by Agent Harper was regarding the discovery of a few abandoned boats, that were the closest link to finding the missing children. There were dozens of children out there, lost and alone, and she could not stop thinking about it and picturing them. Hiding in dark rooms with tears in their eyes, not sure if or when they would be back home.

But the biggest question of all was: when they successfully kidnapped the children, where did they take them? The coast guard had boats and helicopters patrolling all the areas zoned for the recent kidnappings over the last few hours. Nothing had been found as yet. How had the children not been found on boats or islands? Any seaplanes given clearance for take-off would have been noticed and searched, so that wasn't their method of choice for transportation either.

When faced with so many possibilities in an investigation, it is usually best to eliminate them one by one and see which ones you are left with. The children were all kidnapped from schools, on land, and taken to boats in local marinas, each one paired with two handlers. Sometimes one handler brought the boat back to land alone and escaped, but other times the boat was abandoned. Where were the children being dropped off?

There was only one way for people to disappear in the middle of the sea, one last option to consider in this case: submarines.

Chapter Seventeen

"You guys have been looking for hours and you are supposed to be the best of the best!" Sharon exclaimed.

"Honey, they are doing their best, we have to let them do their jobs," Harry comforted although he had to admit that he felt the same way. They seemed to have gathered every law enforcement professional in the United States and Canada to investigate this ring, only to come up with some measly abandoned boats. Life was feeling more and more hopeless every hour without news on Jamie's or the kidnapped kids' whereabouts.

Where could these people hide dozens of scared, loud kids for 24 hours a day, 7 days a week, all at once without raising a single alarm or getting one complaint? Why did they always choose to travel by boat, and with two handlers instead of one? Could they be transporting the kids to an island not yet discovered? And why, if that was the case?

"We are trying our hardest, folks. We're really hoping that the abandoned boats will lead to some answers. There has to be a reason they operate the way they do," said Harper as she ran a hand down her face.

Sharon turned to Harper and saw all her desperation, fear, and frustration mirrored in her face, and immediately felt ashamed of herself. How could she stand there and accuse a woman of not being determined enough to search for her son when she was carrying the weight of all those missing children on her shoulders? She felt tears in her eyes as she hugged Harper, silently acknowledging that they were going through this nightmare together, sharing the long days, sleepless nights, and tears. As she looked up at Harper, she saw that tears were forming in her eyes as well and gave her one last squeeze before she stepped back to stand next to her husband.

"I'm sorry, Harper, I know this must be stressful for you, too. I just miss my son," a sob rose out of Sharon's throat.

"It's alright, ma'am, I know this process can be painful. We really are using every resource we have at our disposal to bring down this ring and bring these kids home safe," Harper said.

"I just hope you solve the case before it's too late – for both Jamie and for those other kids they took," said Harry.

Chapter Eighteen

Stacey had been sitting in the small, suffocating police station for the last two hours, waiting for any word on her daughter's whereabouts. The little makeup that she'd had the time to put on while she was on the way out had streaked down her face and dried hours ago. Her impatience started to boil over again as she started to make her way over to the desk where she initially reported her daughter's disappearance.

"Have you heard anything about my daughter? Her name is Kimberly Jacobs and she has already been missing for hours," Stacey asked the woman working at the front desk.

The receptionist answered, "I'm sorry, ma'am, we've got people out looking for your daughter-" She was cut off mid-sentence by the shrill ring of her phone, which she then answered.

"We found a young girl matching the description provided for Kimberly. I am sending an email with an attached photograph of her over now. We need the mother to confirm that it is her daughter. If she's sure that's her daughter, bring her to Memorial Hospital."

Before she could even utter 'yes ma'am' in response, the officer hung up the phone.

The receptionist turned back to Stacey and said, "Ma'am, I need you to confirm that the young lady in this photo is your daughter," and beckoned her closer so they could see the computer monitor.

"Yes, that's her! Where is she? Is she alright?" Stacey was beyond relieved that her daughter was alive. Tears of happiness began to stream down her face as she imagined her reunion. She would never take her daughter for granted again; she would cherish every second they had together.

"I see her now. We will be on our way soon, sir," an officer spoke into his phone as he headed towards Stacey from of an office in the back. He smiled at Stacey as he removed the phone from his ear and pressed the end call button. When he reached her, he extended his arm and opened his hand for her to shake, and she obliged happily with a big smile on her face.

"Hello, ma'am, I'm Officer Cyrus and I will be escorting you to the hospital to see your daughter this afternoon," said the officer. With a quick 'follow me', he led her to his cruiser and within a matter of minutes they were on their way to the hospital where her daughter was a patient.

About 15 minutes later, they arrived at the hospital and Officer Cyrus immediately escorted Stacey to her daughter's room. Stacey's face lit up as soon as she saw her. Although Kimberly looked as if she was just taking a nap, Stacey knew that her daughter was unconscious. Even with that knowledge at that time, she cringed when she saw the small, red irritated patch on her daughter's skin that indicated that she had been drugged.

"She's one of the lucky ones – she made it back home safe," said Officer Cyrus.

Chapter Nineteen

Harper woke up to the ringtone she had specifically set temporarily to the tone of an alarm clock, so she was assured to always be woken by it ringing. She specifically changed it during this case for one reason – she had been having trouble sleeping, and when she was able to, the loud ringing was barely audible to her. On the rare occasion that she was able to sleep, nightmares about darts and crying children in dark rooms, especially Jamie, woke her only 10 minutes into her power naps.

"Ma'am, he just woke up," the agent said. Harper was extremely proud of the bright junior agent for arresting Kimberly's kidnappers. His first big arrest. He managed to detain two criminals in one of the most notorious cases of organized crime in the last decade, and his name would never be forgotten.

"I'm on my way. Bring both suspects into the interrogation room and do not let anybody you don't know into that room or I will have your badge," replied Harper sternly. Although she was proud of his big arrest, sometimes an agent rising through the ranks and receiving so much attention so quickly needed to be humbled.

She quickly threw on her uniform and grabbed her badge from her bedside table. Was it wrong that this was the most alive that she had felt in months? She loved being in the middle of the action of a case, along with the anticipation that came with getting answers from the lowest of the low. She hated being sidelined when she was a rookie, being told not to interfere and stand in the corner when all she wanted was to take over the handling of the interrogation herself.

She was walking through the old, creaky doorway of the police station 20 minutes later, greeted with 'good morning' from all directions. She smiled and nodded at every officer who greeted her. She had built her career very carefully, always demanding respect and an acknowledgment of her authority from her inferiors, but always showing them the same respect and acknowledging their hard work and dedication. Taking this approach her entire career had always earned her their support and helped her make some genuine lifelong friends.

She walked through the door into the interrogation room and sneered as her eyes fell on the two perpetrators. They both wore smug smiles and were tapping the table with the same simultaneous and monotonous tempo. The man's teeth were filthy. An unhealthy shade of yellow that Harper had never even seen on a human being before, they were uneven and severely chipped. Her eyes moved to the woman and she gasped softly. She was beautiful, the polar opposite of her partner.

"Stop that," Harper snapped, concluding eventually that their consistent tapping was not playing the role of Morse code. Their smug smiles only widened in response. She was momentarily reminded of the Cheshire cat as she watched their smiles grow.

"So, you make your living kidnapping kids for some scumbag?" she asked them. At first, they didn't respond, but when Harper slammed her hand on the table in front of them and yelled, "Answer me," the woman snapped back in a language Harper had no trouble instantly recognizing as Russian. Harper started to ask herself why this Russian woman was helping a kidnapping ring? Then she registered that this was much bigger than they thought – this ring originated in

Russia and may well be operating from within Russia. Her case just became an international issue, and with the tension already high between the United States and Russia, that was very dangerous. Very dangerous, indeed.

That was when she noticed the faint outline of a clear capsule protruding from behind each of their ears. Two Russians trying to kidnap a little girl in the United States, with pills behind their ears immediately after they were captured? It was clear that this interview wasn't going to go anywhere until they found a Russian translator, and maybe not even then.

Harper walked over to the junior agent who was guarding the door and whispered in his ear, "They both have capsules full of cyanide. They are going to try off themselves as soon as this interrogation ends because they are far more afraid of their handlers than they are of us. We can't let that happen, can we?"

"No ma'am," he said with a determined look, much to her delight. He quickly darted over to the Russian prisoners and grabbed the poorly concealed pills from their resting spots behind the ears and handed them to his superior. Harper smiled as they started yelling in Russian, glaring at them with mean eyes, no doubt showering them with every insult they could think of.

"We're done here, thank you for your cooperation," Harper quipped as she walked out of the interviewing room, now the one with a smug smile on her face.

Chapter Twenty

Agent Harper and Detective Boyd nodded at each other as they walked into the secure room designated to meeting about the case. They were joined by all Agent Harper and Detective Boyd's superiors, military personnel, and the Secretary of Defense. They scanned the room for their names and sat down in the seats assigned to them as signified by their name tags on the long oval-shaped table. Harper had just picked up her case briefing packet when the director of the FBI cleared his throat.

"Good morning and welcome. You all know why you are here. We need to secure this ring before they cause an international incident," he said. He scanned the room as he spoke, watching the reactions as he emphasized the international implications of the incident. He was met with nervous expressions from all in attendance who were worried about the latent consequences. –War was the worst-case scenario. The United States and Russia did not need more reason for hostility, walking on eggshells as they already were.

"We have an update on their movements. They started kidnapping children in South America as of last week. Same MO as the other kidnappings – they abduct the kids while they are at recess, quickly and quietly. We need to stop this now, too many kids are missing and too many questions can't be answered. Are there any questions?" asked the director.

"Sir, have we found out which drug they used in the tranquilizer?" the junior officer who arrested the Russians asked and Harper smiled.

He was the only person in the room who was not high-ranking in any law enforcement agency. As the person who had captured the only handlers still in possession of a victim, doors were now opened for him, offering opportunities he would otherwise not have seen for years to come.

"The rookie has a good question! Yes, we have, and we are investigating where they may have purchased it," said the director.

As he opened his mouth to say more, his phone began to vibrate and then went on to ring loudly on the table before him. He huffed in annoyance, but his eyes widened when he saw his phone screen.

He held up a finger as he uttered, "Excuse me, I have to take this."

He cleared his throat and picked up his cell phone with hands trembling slightly.

He answered the call with a, "Hello sir, do we have an update?" and listened intently to everything said on the other end of the line until he eventually hung up.

He turned to everyone in the room with a serious expression and said, "That was the president of the United States. It's time for the American people to know what's happening."

Chapter Twenty-One

The president replaced the receiver having ended his phone call to the director, with a grave look on his face. It was up to him to hold the first press conference on the new kidnapping ring operating throughout the United States and Canada. He had never liked press conferences, but he knew this one was going to be especially hectic. The media would simply not stand for this. He could hear them now: "Children taken in broad daylight from schoolyards. I've never heard of such a thing! How could the teachers let this happen? How could you continue to let this happen?"

Whenever disaster occurs, even the most drastically different of people seem to react similarly; blaming everybody except those who are committing the heinous crimes. When it comes down to it, pointing their fingers at him and blaming him seemed their chosen defense mechanism. As if he would have been able to save those poor children. God knows where they are and what those savages have done to them.

He tried his best to clear his head. He cleared his throat and stepped into the room full of reporters. Every single one of them waiting for his comment so they could twist it into whatever completely different meaning they concocted to that intended. He scanned the room and flinched as the camera flashes went off. He had learned a long time ago, long before he was ever elected president, to look at a room full of people before addressing them and if they see you acknowledge them. It makes them feel more respected and more confident in what you have to say. He was definitely acknowledging them. He seemed to be surrounded by a group of bloodthirsty hounds who wouldn't stop their attack until they had the answers they wanted to hear. God, he hated press conferences.

"Good morning, ladies and gentlemen. I trust you have already heard rumors about all the recent kidnappings being somehow related. Unfortunately, these rumors have merit to them," said the president. The room resounded with gasps and exclamations of surprise, although they had all been quite aware of this information before coming into the conference. He always wondered about the purpose behind them pretending that they were receiving new information. What he knew for sure was that he would probably never know.

"Please settle down. We have reason to believe that the main conspirators behind this operation are from a foreign country. All the criminals we have arrested in connection with this crime speak fluent Russian," he said. He knew ahead of time that the room would be filled with cries of outrage and angry curses when he made this particular announcement, and he assumed correctly. One woman even spat on the floor, which frankly was a little excessive, in his opinion.

"They have only targeted children during school recess so far, and only children sitting by themselves. We have to make sure that we are keeping our children as safe as possible by keeping them together in groups whenever they are out of the classroom, no matter where they are going or the time of day," he announced.

He took a deep breath and then said, "As of yesterday one of the girls has been returned safely home to her mother." He anticipated he would be met with applause even before they started clapping. They may very well have thrived off negative information, but they could nonetheless not help but be grateful for the recovery of a child. The smile that had grown on his face disappeared as soon as it had come when he prepared his next announcement.

"Although it is wonderful that we reunited one family, there are still dozens of broken families out there that need answers and want their children back. We are continuing to investigate and will hold another conference when we have further updates. Thank you and have a nice day. "Walking out of the room, he felt the familiar relief that comes only at the conclusion of a press conference.

He turned to his aide who was walking with and gravely said, "We have to find those kids before there is nothing left of them to find."

Chapter Twenty-Two

Stacey leaned forward in the seat that she had hours ago relocated to beside her daughter's hospital bed. She was getting more worried about Kimberly by the second. Was she supposed to be slipping in and out of consciousness at this point? She squeezed her hand, silently wishing that it would bring her daughter out of her prolonged unconsciousness and see her smile at her. Her heart started to beat like a drum when her daughter's hand began to twitch under hers, and her eyes widened in surprise.

Kimberly looked up and whimpered, "Mommy?"

"Honey? I'm here, Mommy's here."

Kimberly slowly opened her eyes and when she saw her mother, tears started to well in her eyes. Stacey gently wrapped her arms around her daughter, wishing she could hold her in her arms every minute of every day for all eternity. One thing was for sure. She was never losing her daughter again. She would take her out of the school and transfer her to one she trusted. Or even homeschool her, if that's what it came to.

She suddenly remembered that she promised to call Officer Cyrus the second Kimberly woke up and started talking. She pulled his card out of her purse and carefully dialed his number.

"She's awake, she just woke up and started talking to me," she blurted. She was sure to add the fact that she had spoken having already called 3 times before today. Three times that had turned out to be false alarms.

"I'm on my way now, Stacey. Keep her talking and comfortable," the officer blurted, the sound of rustling in the background as he picked up the key to his cruiser. Ending the phone call, she gently caressed Kimberly's face.

"How are you feeling, sweetie?"

"My head hurts, Mommy. Can we go home?" asked Kimberly, whimpering as she spoke.

"Not yet, baby, a nice man is going to come and ask you questions. After we talk to him, we have to wait for the nurse to say that it's alright."

Officer Cyrus entered Kimberly's hospital room, interrupting the small talk between mother and daughter. Stacey had not wanted to over extend her before the questioning began. The officer smiled and nodded at her and then extended his hand out to her daughter.

"You must be Kimberly! I've heard so much about you from your mom," he spoke as she reached for his hand and shook it. Then she waved her hand and tried to hide her face behind her mom's hand. She had always been nervous around strangers, even before this recent ordeal.

"Do you remember anything from the last day, sweetie?" he asked. When he saw the look of confusion dawn on her face, he already knew what was coming.

"I don't remember, I'm sorry," Kimberly sobbed as her mother held her and whispered sweet words of reassurance in her ear.

Chapter Twenty-Three

During the drive back to the station Harper tried to wrap her mind around the idea of the ring kidnapping even more kids from new places. The director was right, there were too many unanswered questions and too many people looking to them for answers for them to not have any to give. At that point, the president had to get involved. Hopefully, Sharon and Harry hadn't seen his press conference yet. She wanted to be the one to tell them about finding Kimberly.

She sighed and momentarily closed her eyes and rested her head on the steering wheel before taking the keys out of the ignition. As she climbed out of the car, she couldn't stop thinking about the news she was just given, imagining what it would be like when the number of missing children rose into the hundreds. Why were these people kidnapping innocent children, and what did they want? She was still trying to come up with answers as she walked into the police station.

Sharon immediately stood when she saw Harper walk into the room, and blurted out, "What happened? Did you find him?" The desperation in her eyes and her voice almost brought Harper to tears; this woman was depending on her to bring her son home safe and sound, and she wasn't even sure if she was capable of taking care of herself at that point.

When Harry saw the look on Harper's face, he grabbed his wife's hand before she even had a chance to answer, and said, "I don't think so, honey. Not yet."

Harper could see him losing more and more hope every time she saw him. Losing hope of ever seeing his son again and in the justice system as a whole; losing hope that Harper could do her job.

"We didn't find Jamie, but we did find another student being held captive by two criminals, and we have detained them." said Harper. Although this wasn't the news that they were hoping for, a glimmer of hope shone in their eyes and Harper knew why; they would finally get some answers. After so many sleepless nights, wondering if their son was dead or alive, they would finally find out what these people wanted with him What they were doing and what they were planning to do with him.

"She is unconscious in the hospital right now, but one of our agents will ask her questions as soon as she wakes up." Harper assured them.

Sharon stepped forward towards Harper as she said, "Thank you for everything you have done for us. I don't know what we would have done if we didn't have you in our corner."

She had such a genuine smile on her face that it made Harper's sides ache. There was a real possibility that this woman would never see her son again and that it would break both their hearts. That was one of her rules. No getting personally invested in a case. Especially one like this, where the light at the end of the tunnel seemed not to exist and they would be in the dark forever.

"Of course, ma'am," replied Harper, having to make a conscious effort to keep her voice from shaking. As she smiled back at Sharon, she couldn't help feeling guilty. They had no idea where her son was or what was being done to him, and they probably wouldn't for a while.

"We are seeing a consistent pattern of two abductors taking the children onto boats that have been abandoned at sea. When they return the boat to a different marina, the children and one of the perpetrators are gone," said Harper. She was met with two expressions of confusion and continued with the update she was permitted to give them.

"At this point, we are unsure where the children are being taken to or dropped off. It honestly just seems like they are being dropped into the middle of the ocean." "Maybe they are being held in another larger boat until their captors have enough for whatever they are planning. Then they could be transporting them to an island or crossing the US border," offered Harry. One look into his desperate, tired eyes clearly indicated just how close to snapping he was and how near he was to a breakdown. That was assuming he hadn't had one already.

"Maybe," said Harper, trying to sound as confident as possible, even though she doubted that his theory was accurate. She already had a theory of her own, but yet another of her rules was never to share unconfirmed information with anyone. This could not only get her into trouble, but also hurt them if she was wrong. Sharing inaccurate information could be dangerous.

"There are very few ways they could be holding the kids after they have been dropped off in the ocean. They would need a place for them to eat and sleep and living quarters where they can also avoid detection," Harper thought out loud. Sharon shook her head and ran her hand down her face in frustration, failing to figure out what Harper was implying.

"Sharon, Harry, I think you guys should sleep in a hotel tonight. It is unsafe to keep sleeping at your house. They could know where you live and have you under surveillance or even attack you," warned Harper.

"We have to stay. What if Jamie escapes and comes home?" asked Sharon, the desperation returning to her voice.

Harry squeezed his wife's hand, "Honey, maybe she's right. It could be dangerous to stay at our house, and we won't be any good to Jamie if these people make us disappear too."

Sharon nodded as tears filled her eyes, and she turned to her husband.

"You're right," she agreed.

"We'll go to a hotel for now, if that's what you think would be best, Harper," she whispered.

Harper smiled in response to her consent and thanked her for agreeing.

"You won't regret it, ma'am, a hotel is the safest place for you to be living right now."

"Call me Sharon."

Chapter Twenty-Four

"Detain all who are in your custody and have them taken to the location, and use the protocol we discussed," the president instructed over the phone. He made sure to disclose the location to the director in private because their phone line could easily be tapped, especially if the head of this ring was Russian. They were notorious for hacking into phones from across international waters, and their hackers would have no problem listening in to the president's phone calls.

After hearing the beeping sound that indicated the end of the phone call, he set his phone down on his desk and audibly sighed in exasperation. The same questions had been running through his head since he had attended the first briefing on this case.

Who were these people? What did they want with these innocent children they were kidnapping? Although one question in particular refused to leave the forefront of his mind; was this a Russian tactic to goad him into declaring war?

If it was, it would not work. Although this case was serious, he was not going to allow millions of US civilians and soldiers to be murdered in another war. Although the United States would probably eventually win, too many lives would be lost on both sides for him to ever be able to live with the decision.

The 'protocol' they had discussed was to use any resource at their disposal to get the Russians to talk. If it took torture, truth serum, a lie detector, or simply effective interrogative techniques, he would not walk into the next press conference without additional information.

During his campaign and consequent election, he always promised the American people one thing and that was that he would be effective by whatever means necessary. His legacy would be one to be respected for the right answers, not for cheating on his wife or making unfair treaties and agreements with other countries. He would be fair to countries who treated the US fairly, and harsh and swift with those who disrespected and threatened the US.

The manner in which this case was handled would no doubt partly shape his legacy and prove to be among his most remembered achievements. They needed answers and they needed them quickly.

"The transfer of the prisoners was successful. They wouldn't talk with normal interrogation methods, but we have resorted to the other strategies we discussed, and they are responding. We are about to gain more intel on this case," the director said in a phone call some two hours later.

Chapter Twenty-Five

Jamie groaned softly as his eyes slowly opened and he scanned his surroundings. He rubbed his eyes and looked around again. Where was he? He felt sluggish and it was a chore to even keep his eyes open long enough to get a clear view of the room.

"They must have injected me with another needle," he thought. He was getting used to the feeling of being constantly drugged and waking up in strange places.

He remembered when his parents had taken him on a trip to Florida and told him they would be flying in an airplane. He wasn't even entirely sure what an airplane was, but when they were boarding, he felt the panic set in. They were traveling in a huge machine with wings. In the sky for hours. Just thinking about all the potential disasters that could occur made his stomach hurt. Could this be an airplane? He certainly felt the same panic and, from what he was able to make out, there were similarities.

Then he saw them – sets of bunk beds all around the room already occupied by other children, all of who were asleep. He tried to focus well enough to count the number of bunk beds, but he couldn't. Dozens of kids were sleeping in the room. As he continued scanning the room, his eyes stopped on a tall woman holding a gun in her hand. He turned towards her and squinted to the point he thought she might be unable to tell that he was awake.

She turned her head to the side as another guard came into view who silently imparted some communication in sign language. Jamie had seen people use American sign language and this was not it. They were communicating using sign language from another country. He felt another wave of fear as he came to the realization that these people were not from the United States. The people who had kidnapped all these children were from a foreign country, but which one?

He suddenly realized that his bladder was full and that he had to use the bathroom. As the second guard left the room, he considered asking the woman watching them if he could use the bathroom, but he changed his mind. He was far too scared to get her attention, let alone ask for anything, especially seeing that she was holding a gun. He decided to hold it in until he had an opportunity to ask someone else or until she left the room, which was unlikely. He resigned himself to the fact that he would probably have to go to the bathroom right there, on that uncomfortable bed.

What happened to lead him to this point from sitting on the playground to being locked in a room full of kids with a gun trained on him? If he wasn't even safe sitting alone in the corner of a playground, could he ever be safe anywhere? He thought about how frantic his parents must be – their son having vanished from school during recess without so much as a sign of him since. No ransom call, no demands, no answers. After he felt the prick in his neck at recess, he vaguely remembered waking up in a strange car with strangers, and now waking up here.

Too many blocks of time were unaccounted for since that day on the playground. Was the car a dream, just the result of the drugs he was being injected with or was it all real? He was still contemplating what was fake and what was reality when he gave in to sleep, allowing his eyes to close.

Jamie felt himself start to come to again as he licked his dry and cracked lips, craving water. He slowly realized that he still needed to use the bathroom and he couldn't hold it in. It was either happening in the bathroom or right there in that bed. After taking a few minutes to build up the courage, he was prepared to ask the woman where he should go to find a toilet.

"Where is the b-bathroom?" he stuttered. She immediately whipped her head in his direction when she heard his voice and sneered at him. He cowered on his bunk as she slowly walked towards him, seemingly getting angrier with every step. When she reached him, she gripped his arm tightly and started dragging him across the metal floor while he tripped over his own feet trying to stay upright.

She finally released him in front of a short white door which she opened, pushing him towards the doorway. He was still looking around inside the dark room when the guard switched the light on and slammed the door behind him. He suddenly remembered that the airplane he had flown on to Florida also had a toilet. Did they bring him on another plane? While using the bathroom facilities, he looked at the walls and saw odd words and symbols he had never seen before. He shook it off and walked out of the bathroom, immediately coming face-to-face with the guard.

"Where did you take me? Where are my mommy and daddy?" he exclaimed while she stared at him with disdain in response.

"Go," she said in a very strange accent and pushed him out of the doorway and towards the room full of bunk beds. He allowed himself to be led to his bunk and there he lay down. He felt both relief and a fresh bout of fear wash simultaneously over him as he lay down and allowed sleep to carry him away again.

Chapter Twenty-Six

"Is it true that we have new information?" asked the FBI director as he quickly scanned the room for bugs, as was his norm. Even though some rooms were supposedly secure, crazier things had happened than merely a breach. This case was gaining traction, creating a global issue, just as they feared it would. He looked around the table and put the names of the agencies to faces; the CIA, Homeland Security, the Coast Guard, and even some unfamiliar faces.

"Yes, we have obtained a satellite video that we believe shows the movements of this ring," the head of the CIA said.

The television mounted on the wall in the front of the room suddenly came to life and everybody turned to face it. There was a grainy image of the beginning of a video showing a boat on the ocean.

"Was there a child on this boat?" asked the director of the Coast Guard, with a grimace.

The head of the CIA replied, "Yes, to our knowledge, a child was on this boat at the time this footage was caught."

He silently nodded and pressed play on the remote in his hand.

The video began with the boat silently speeding along the water for a few seconds and then suddenly coming to a halt in the middle of the open sea. Then a woman appeared, carrying a motionless child and handing him off to a person that was outside of the camera's view. It looked like she was dropping the child into the sea, but there was no way they would risk getting caught only to kill them in the long run. Everyone in the room seemed to have the same confused expression and to be thinking the same thing; what was going on here?

"Submarines have been identified on both the East and West coast, both being used to store these children and to stay on the move deep under water to avoid detection." He cleared his throat and continued, "We have reliable intel that they are using stolen boats to meet their handlers in the gulf-of-Mexico. They are following a pattern here and we have finally figured it out, now we need to find the kids."

He continued, "Judging by the position of this sighting, we are assuming they are headed towards South America. They could have gone just about anywhere, but we think that they most likely went to a country that can be reached by submarine."

"My god, Harper was right," muttered the director of the FBI.

A grave look crossed his face as he said, "We have another video that you need to see from a few months ago."

He pressed the play button for a second time and a video played showing a group of kids sitting on the deck of a boat surrounded by armed guards who were scanning the perimeter.

After he stopped the video and turned off the television, he flicked the light switch back on and looked around the room. He was met with scared and confused faces which now looked even more determined to catch these people.

"This is footage from the Panama kidnappings, and although the children were taken by boat rather than a submarine, we have strong reason to suspect that these two cases are related. We believe that these victims were taken to Columbia to either be sold into the sex-trade or be illegally adopted by rich families." "We also believe that these kids will meet the same fate if we do not find them. Relay all this information to your agents and find them." he said with a sense of urgency.

Chapter Twenty-Seven

Harry reached for his nightstand to press the snooze button on his blaring alarm clock. He ran his hand down his face and he was filled with dread, internally preparing to face another day without his son. He gently climbed out of bed, trying not to fully wake his wife.

"Go back to bed, sweetie," he whispered when he saw her start to stir. She grabbed his hand for a few seconds and then turned her back to him.

He slicked his hair back on his way to the bathroom and rinsed his face in the sink. Later, he washed his hands and softly closed the door. As he walked to the kitchen, his thoughts were on his morning coffee. Coffee had become somewhat of an antidote whenever he was hurting. Taking the first sip, he checked his voicemails and text messages for any updates. He was disappointed but not surprised to find neither.

He grabbed a notepad and pencil from the breakfast table and began his to-do list for the day. That was how he had been getting through the last few days. Writing a list of things to do helped him get through the hard days. He gripped the pencil tightly as he carefully wrote 'Contact Panama police.'

"Good morning, honey," said Sharon as she hugged her husband from behind. They both savored the sweet moment in the middle of the chaos for a few seconds.

"Good morning," Harry replied as he turned towards her to see tears starting to pool in her eyes.

"They are never going to find him, Harry. He disappeared days ago, and they haven't brought our baby back to us yet." "Don't say that, honey. They will find him; they're doing their best. They already have so many different leads that they are following. We will always keep looking, no matter what happens," Harry assured his wife. As his wife turned to him with a hopeful look on her face, he squeezed her hand, reassuring her that he would always be there.

"We will never stop," she replied in agreement. "I'm so glad that they have made so much progress so quickly. Finding Jamie seemed so impossible when he first disappeared. Thank God a nine-year-old boy disappearing into thin air brought everybody on the right side of the law together."

"They have made so much progress in so little time. I have a feeling that the connection between this case and the Panama abductions could be the key to solving this case. I know it has been three days already, but they will find him. We will find him, honey," he replied.

Their conversation was cut short when Harry's phone screen lit up with Agent Harper's name and rang. He answered the call and immediately put it on speaker so his wife could hear what Harper had to say.

"Hello, Harry. I have good news and bad news," said Harper nervously. Tears started to well up in Sharon's eyes when she heard the last few words, and Harry grabbed her hand, silently offering his support and presence.

"I'll give you the bad news first. There are no more updates on the locations of the submarines; they could be anywhere at this point. We also have definite confirmation that the drug used on the girl is from Russia. We were holding out hope that the ring hadn't originated in Russia, but it is already affecting foreign relations." Harry looked into his wife's eyes and knew that they were both just thankful that they hadn't found their son's body. The fact that they had lost track of the submarines was discouraging, but at least he was still presumed to be on it.

"The good news is that I was able to get that phone number we discussed. I will text you the number of the lead investigator of the Panama abduction cases after this phone call. Hopefully, he can help shed light on the solution for all of us," finished Harper.

"Thank you so much," said Sharon.

"Of course. I will update you if there are more changes," Harper added before hanging up.

A few minutes after the call ended, he received the text from Harper with the detective's phone number and immediately wrote it down on his list. As soon as he set his pencil down, he picked up his phone and dialed the number.

He shared a hopeful look with his wife as the phone rang – once, twice, and then stopped.

"This is Detective Ramos." "This is Harry and Sharon, Jamie's parents. Harper said she would tell you about us ahead of time. Please tell me you can help us find our son," begged Harry.

Chapter Twenty-Eight

Jamie's eyes hesitantly opened once again and he scanned his surroundings, trying to figure out whether or not he had been moved again. His eyes stopped on the familiar bunk beds that filled the room. He was definitely in the same place that he had fallen asleep. He turned to the bunk across from him and rubbed his eyes to help him focus. He gasped when he realized children were no longer asleep on the other bunks.

He turned in the bed to go back to sleep, when he was suddenly jerked upright, face-to-face with the odd-looking woman who had kidnapped him. She took him by the shoulder and pushed him towards a man he had never seen before. The man squeezed his shoulder and gently pushed him down a strange corridor with a metal floor, following behind armed with a hand gun.

Metal floors were everywhere. This wasn't like the airplane he remembered. He turned to face the man halfway down the corridor and felt an odd semblance of peace. For the first time in days he was finally with someone who wasn't yelling at him, hurting him, or poking him with needles.

"We see other kids now," the heavily accented man announced similarly to the accents Jamie had been hearing among the others.

Jamie immediately scanned the room as he was pushed over the threshold into a new area. Then he saw them – all the kids he had seen on the first night who had been asleep in the bunks, and then some, all sitting on a carpet together. They all seemingly turned their heads towards him when he walked into the room. At first, he thought they were looking at him, but when he turned around as well, it was to see a smiling woman carrying juice boxes and peanut butter and jelly sandwiches. He felt his stomach start to rumble as he asked for a sandwich, his voice just part of a sea of pleas around the room. After he gulped down two juice boxes and two sandwiches, he felt full and comfortable enough to ask questions.

"Where are we?" he asked the man, who had led him into the room, only to be met with a silent response.

"Do you guys know where we are?" he asked the other children, but they didn't have answers for him either. He was met with wide confused eyes and murmurs of, 'I don't know.'

"I have an announcement," the strangely accented man addressed everyone from the front of the room. All heads turned to him as he spoke, all waiting for the answers they had been longing for.

"You will get off soon and get on a boat, then see your parents," he continued.

Chapter Twenty-Nine

"There it is! Flash our lights at them and give them a chance to surrender," commanded the Fleet Admiral.

The pride he felt at that moment was impossible to explain. His crew had been the first to find a submarine. Although he did warn them not to use force immediately, he secretly wished that they could. Who did these people think they were, coming into his country and terrorizing the nation? They had been so meticulous and careful to avoid getting caught, but they were about to feel the consequences of their actions.

It was a miracle that they were able to detect the submarine in the first place as it fled to Russia, which is why they were in a hurry, presumably. They were not expecting one of their puppets to be captured, and it scared them. So here they were, cornered trying to escape using the long route around the tip of South America. More games – they loved playing games.

"Fire, but do not directly hit it, there are children on board," he said as they shot one torpedo into the dark sea directly under the submarine. And then it started. The sub started moving faster, trying to get away, and he smiled. Now they were really getting started.

"After them," he screamed, spotting the cave they were headed to before the others did. They noticed too late to avoid it or stop and the sub kept going, straight into their trap.

"Surrender now, there is no escape. We have you cornered. Rise to the surface or we will have to use deadly force," he demanded over the radio.

"You will not do it with children on board," replied a man in a clear Russian accent.

"Show them just how serious we are. Only shoot at the side. Do not do enough damage to harm anyone onboard," the Admiral instructed his crew.

The torpedo hit the side of the submarine, and the Russian urged, "Stop this! We are coming up, do not shoot anymore!"

As the foreign submarine began to rise to the surface, so did they, readying their firearms in the event of a worst-case scenario. A shootout.

A sniper on top of the boat aimed his firearm at the opening of the submarine as it surfaced, and the door slowly opened. A man emerged off a ladder and put his hands in the air as he stepped onto the slick surface of the submarine.

"Go, go, go! Find those kids," the admiral commanded.

"Get everyone into the conference room and put me on camera, it's time to tell them what we found," commanded the officer.

As the conference room filled again with officials, the stress and tension were like a dark cloud over all. They had all the important information for this case and the need for its urgency, but they had yet to yield any actual results. The director hated to admit it, but they were good at what they did. Avoiding detection once again, just when the Coast Guard thought they had them backed into a corner was no easy feat.

The desperation for answers was shown on every single face in the room; everybody hoping somebody else had found something. When somebody at the front of the room loudly cleared their throat, everybody focused their attention to the front of the room and the television screen showing a representative of the US Navy appearing from within a secure room.

"We found a submarine maneuvering around the tip of South America on its way to Russia. The vessel has surfaced, and we are currently waiting for the all-clear. CIA and Homeland personnel need to get here now," he declared amidst a round of applause in response.

"Don't celebrate too soon. This isn't over just yet. At least one submarine is still out there, maybe two. We are questioning the prisoners, but they are hard to break. This will not end until all the kids are found and every single man and woman in this ring are put behind bars. Keep working."

Chapter Thirty

"So many children were kidnapped and never found. We searched for months but it was as if they had simply vanished into thin air. There was no trace of them or any solid leads to follow," Harry's heart sank at the detective's admission. They never found them, and they had just given up. Is that what would happen with his son?

"We are confident that these cases are related and with these new leads, we are also confident that we will find all the children missing from the three countries," assured detective Ramos.

"Thank you very much, detective," Harry said. Sharon stared, transfixed on the phone, her mind running a million miles an hour to process what she had just heard.

"Of course, sir. We will find your son and prosecute these people to the fullest extent of the law; that is a promise." Sharon squeezed her husband's hand, filled with renewed hope. Another country added to the search.

As Harry hung up, he managed to force a smile for the sake of his wife. They gave up in Panama, would they give up here if they didn't find the answers they were looking for? No matter how many assurances he got from agents or detectives, he had no guarantee that they would find his son.

Then it hit him like a semi-truck: he had to help in person. He would never be able to live with himself if he wasn't there doing all he could to help find his son.

"Honey, I have to help them to find our son. I can't just sit around here while he is out there, scared and alone," Harry said. He gently took his wife's hand with a sad but determined look in his eyes.

"Don't do this, Harry. Let the police do their job. They are trained for this and they know how to find our son," begged Sharon.

"I'm going, Sharon. You need to stay here in case Jamie comes home. The cops have to follow the law. I will do whatever it takes; break whatever rule I need to."

"No way I'll let you go alone. I'm going with. My sister can watch the house and stay updated with the police here. She will take care of things," Sharon decided.

"Are you sure you want to do this?" Harry asked hesitantly.

"I want to find our son as much as you do, and I am willing to sacrifice anything," Sharon said with silent tears streaming down her face.

They went to their room and got the suitcases out of their closet, packing for a month. Who knew how long they would be away? After packing, they carried their bags to Harry's car, climbed in and pulled out of the driveway, making their way to the airport.

Ten minutes and one tense car ride later, they arrived at the airport, parked and walked inside where Harry made a beeline for the long queue to buy tickets while Sharon walked over to an indoor café to get coffee. Waiting in line, she had the feeling someone was staring at the back of her head. Turning to confront it, she was met with a line of chattering people, none of whom were looking in her direction.

She turned around and ran her hand down her face. Since when was she this paranoid? She felt it again, somebody staring at her, watching her every move. She quickly whipped her head around and saw a man trying to duck out of her view. She left the queue to confront him; could this man be involved in Jamie's kidnapping? They were following her now, on top of everything else.

"Stop right there," she yelled as she grabbed his shoulder and spun him around to face her. She was met with the terrified, pale face of a teenage boy.

"Please stop! I just saw you on the news and wanted some cash for a photo," he begged. Tears started to well in his eyes in fear as Sharon regained control of herself and let go of his shoulder.

"I'm so sorry, I thought you were somebody else," she apologized. She watched the kid run away and out of the building as she bit down on her lip.

What were they doing to her? What was this case turning her into?

Chapter Thirty-One

The Admiral turned his head to the sound of his officer announcing the all-clear and walking back to their boat. He watched the officer approaching to update him.

"Sir, we only found handlers on board, no sign of any children," the officer admitted. He was met with an angry huff from the admiral and groans from his fellow officers.

"They all seem to have ingested cyanide. Most are dead, but some are still holding on, but not for much longer."

"I have called in Homeland and the CIA to search the vessel. They'll find anything there is to find," the admiral announced.

After about half an hour of silence and anxious waiting, the crew was rewarded by the sound of a helicopter bringing in Homeland and the CIA. The specialists climbed down a ladder onto the submarine and proceeded to process the scene inside and find hidden evidence.

"We will find every shred of evidence that there is to find down there, don't worry," assured the head of the CIA.

"Nothing will be missed. We will find something, anything that leads us to them," added the representative for Homeland Security.

"Ma'am, there is evidence that they were on board, but nothing indicating when and where they were taken," the CIA agent offered.

The Fleet Admiral dialed the cell number of the director of the FBI to update him and anxiously listened as his phone rang.

"We have an update," he said immediately when the director answered.

"All the other men and women we found are dead, most likely poisoned themselves upon discovery. No children were on board, but there was evidence of their presence at some point. We need to keep this quiet for now or else the American people will only be discouraged." The director responded, "I understand. I will update my agents and we will do everything in our power to prevent a leak."

"Thank you, I will keep you updated," promised the Admiral.

As the phone call ended, the director called Harper into his office to update her on the case. She walked in with a glimmer of hope in her eyes and sat down with her hands clasped, hoping for good news.

"They found a submarine. The men and women on board were all found dead or dying as a result of poisoning, and all the children were gone. I need you to keep this confidential, Harper," said the director.

"Yes, sir. Thank you for the update," replied Harper as she left his office. She took a deep breath, fully appreciating that she was about to risk her job by making this phone call, but he deserved to know.

She dialed Harry's phone number and anxiously waited for it to be answered. Although they hadn't found his son, he had the right to any information pertinent to the case, confidential or not.

"Harry, I shouldn't be telling you this but there has been an update in the case."

Chapter Thirty-Two

Jamie scanned his surroundings as the man who had brought him into the room along with other kids gently lifted him up and set him onto the surface of whatever it was that he had been traveling in. He was now certain it wasn't an airplane; Airplanes didn't float in the sea. He felt a sense of hopelessness at not recognizing what it was he was standing on.

He was shoved into the group of kids already out there when he heard the roar of an approaching motor. Could he dare assume that help was on its way? After the ordeal he had been through over the last few days, it had become hard to imagine the cavalry, so to say, coming to his rescue.

"Vamos, Vamos," a bald man with a Spanish accent commanded the children as he rushed them to the edge of the submarine.

Jamie turned around to find that the nice man who had brought him up the stairs was gone, and his heart sank. He scanned his surroundings to see only anxious faces of many guards, all armed and pushing the kids towards the left side of the submarine. When he was pushed closer to the front of the group, he saw a boat idling beside the submarine.

"Vamos!" the woman on the boat angrily encouraged the men helping the children over the side rail and into the vessel.

The guards responded with heightened sense of urgency and began lifting the children and setting them down on the deck of the boat to be herded together in the cabin below. Jamie felt himself being lifted and whimpered as he was released and then pulled down the ladder.

Although he was terrified, he couldn't help but feel relieved and even a sense of excitement. He would see his parents again! Just a few days away from them had seemed like a lifetime of separation. He felt himself starting to smile in spite of himself; he was finally going to see them again. They would know how to make him feel better; they always had.

"There's no reason to smile, they are lying," said one of the boys already onto the boat, a scowl etched into his face.

"Really?" Jamie whimpered as tears started to form in his eyes.

"We've been kidnapped, and nothing has changed. We will never see our parents again," replied the boy with pity in his eyes.

Jamie felt the tears spill over and slide down his face as he realized that the boy was probably telling the truth. Why would these people go to all this trouble just to bring them back in the end? They weren't returning him to his parents, and he was still in danger. He sighed and decided to just rest for a minute.

Jamie's eyes flew open as the guards on the boat started yelling in Spanish and frantically lifting and depositing kids. With a sharp intake of breath, he felt himself being lifted up, exhaling only when he was released and set back down. He felt a guard's hand on his back and surveyed the area on which he stood. He whipped his head towards the sound of an engine and saw a big truck approaching.

As he contemplated how far he could get or if they would use deadly force if he ran, he felt a guard grab his waist from behind. He whipped around to see that the back of the truck was now open and crying kids were being forced physically into it. He scurried into a dark corner by himself in an attempt to claim some measure of personal space.

A few minutes later, a loud slam reverberated the load body as a guard glared at them before pulling a heavy metal door down on the back of the truck. They were instantly enveloped in darkness as the truck pulled out into the street and drove away.

Only a few hours later, Jamie felt as if they had been traveling for days. They were all sweating and had become increasingly dehydrated during the uncomfortable journey. They had stopped once to allow the kids opportunity to use the bathroom. Some kids had probably lied just to get a whiff of fresh air. Maybe they even thought they would be able to summon help, which proved to be an impossible feat at that point.

Jamie tried as hard as he could to focus on the situation at hand, but it was hard when all that consumed his mind was thoughts of water. He had no idea where he was, and he seemed to have more sweat on his skin than saliva in his mouth. As he tried to formulate a useless escape plan just to pass the time, he felt himself once again succumbing to sleep, and he finally gave in.

Chapter Thirty-Three

"We've landed, honey," Sharon shook Harry's arm to wake him.

Harry slowly opened his eyes and looked around the plane, confused by the many smiling faces. How could these people be happy when so many innocent children were missing? Not only children in other countries, their own children, too. But they had dismissed it as if it was of no consequence whatsoever. As if, since they had been unable to solve the case at the time, it somehow became pointless to pursue the matter further.

He made the conscious decision to overlook his view of the situation as his wife took a hold his hand and helped him to stand up. He softly squeezed her hand as they walked down the aisle and exited the plane together. Having recovered their luggage, they saw a man carrying a sign that read, 'Harry and Sharon'. They approached him and when he spoke, they recognized his voice from their phone call.

"What I'm about to tell you is classified, but you deserve to know," Detective Ramos whispered to them. They shook their heads with serious expressions, trying their best to show him that they understood the gravity of the situation.

"We have a list of names of people that you can speak to for answers," he said as he slipped Harry a folded piece of paper.

"You will have to –" Ramos attempted before he was cut off by Harry's cell phone loudly ringing.

"This is Harper, I have to take this. It could be an update on Jamie. I'm sorry," Harry insisted. The detective nodded in understanding as Harry accepted the call.

"Harry, we have a new theory. We think that they are taking the children back to Columbia to be sold as sex slaves or to be illegally adopted by rich families," Harper explained.

Harry's stopped breathing as he silently prayed that Jamie was being sold to a rich family so that he didn't have to consider the implications of the alternative.

"Thank you for the update. I have to go," replied Harry. After he ended the phone call, he nodded to his wife meaningfully and turned to address detective Ramos.

"That was Harper. We have to get to Columbia as soon as possible, but is it still alright if we follow up with all the people on this list?" Harry asked, holding up the folded page.

"Of course," replied Detective Ramos.

Harry turned to his wife and said, "We need to find these people and question them as soon as we can. I'll explain later, but right now we need to buy tickets to Columbia."

Chapter Thirty-Four

Jamie was shaken awake once again by a stone-faced guard who then jerked him into the air by his arm and then set him back on his feet. He felt the guard's hand on his back, guiding him to the edge of the truck's load body. His arms were yanked, and he was once again set down. He tried to look around in the dark, and his eyes focused on the building into which the kids were being pushed.

The armed guards on either side of the double doors were watching the children, probably to scare them just enough to stop them from trying to run. But would they really fire on them if it came down to it? Shoot innocent, scared kids who were just desperate to see their parents again?

While contemplating that, he was pushed through the doorway of the building, following the other kids into a room with the word 'Kindergarten' displayed on the door. Faced with dozens of sleeping pads spread out throughout the room, he was led towards one and pushed to sit-down. Once all the kids were seated on their own mats, two guards left the room, leaving the other two on either side of the doorway, constantly scanning the room.

The guards returned, one carrying a box of juice cartons and the other peanut butter and jelly sandwiches. They moved through the room, handing each child a juice box and a sandwich. All too soon the children were all drinking and eating as if they hadn't eaten in days, which was very likely in most cases.

As time went by, most of the kids either cried themselves to sleep or fell asleep as soon as they put their heads down on their assigned mat. Jamie scanned the room and saw an older boy still awake next to him. When he saw Jamie turn his head towards him, he tried to feign sleep, but Jamie saw that his eyes were open before he did so.

"I know you're awake, you don't have to pretend," whispered Jamie.

"Alright, then. My name is Dan, what is yours?"

"Jamie," he whispered sadly.

"Well, Jamie, I have no idea where we are, but I think I can find out."

"How? They aren't speaking English," asked Jamie.

"I know that, silly. I speak Spanish and I can hear them through the walls if I stay quiet enough," Dan offered by way of explanation.

"Yes! Please tell me what they are saying about us," Jamie said excitedly.

"Shhh! You'll get us caught. I must listen now," Dan said putting a finger to his lips to signal for Jamie to be quiet. He closed his eyes and they both held their breath, listening to them talk, and Dan started translating.

"We will only stay at this school for one night. Some people will come here tomorrow to look at us," Dan whispered, clearly terrified.

Jamie felt the terror on Dan's face reflected on his own as he discovered what the guards were saying about them. Who was coming to see them tomorrow? And why did they need to look at them?

Chapter Thirty-Five

Two boys pushed open a heavy door and stepped out of the room into the streets of Cartagena, Columbia, looking to the sky in wonder, as if they hadn't seen it in months. The two boys ran down the street as if their lives depended on it and came to a halt in front of a police officer.

"We are from Panama, taken by bad people. We escaped," the oldest boy frantically explained with his arm around the younger boy.

The officer looked at them dismissively and said, "Go back to your parents, this is not funny." He assumed they were just delinquents trying to prank them, and turned his back to them, signaling for them to leave.

They walked around to face him, and the younger boy said, "Please, we are in danger and we do not know where we are."

The officer seemed to register the looks of terror on their faces and took their rant more seriously. It registered that they pronounced their words differently and that they had foreign accents.

He turned to them with a serious expression and asked, "What happened to you?"

The youngest boy spoke up in response, "We were taken from the street in Panama months ago. They took us to a hotel here where bad men hurt us."

The officer took them down to the station to be held until further notice, having reported the crime. The sergeant called him into his office a few minutes later and told him to leave the kids in the waiting room.

"The CIA caught on to this case quickly; they are on an emergency flight right now and they will be here shortly. Organize a team for a raid on the hotel immediately. This case is becoming much more public than it was ever supposed to be," the sergeant addressed the officer.

The assembled task team together with the officers arrived outside the doors of the shabby, run-down hotel identified by the boys. They formed a line on either side of the doors and the head of the team signaled for them to wait.

"This is the police. Open the door or we will have to use force," he announced with the help of a megaphone. When he was met with silence, he signaled to his team to use force to get in.

In a coordinated act, they kicked in the double doors and entered the building with their weapons drawn and at the ready. An officer found and turned on the light switch, and they were bathed in light. They searched the rooms to find meals not eaten and suitcases in the process of being packed.

The head of the team cursed, "They must have started packing when they realized the kids were missing. They were tipped off before we got here, and now they are in the wind."

He relinquished his gun in favor of the walkie talkie from his belt and said, "Question the kids and then bring them back to where they were taken from."

Harper walked out of the meeting with a grim look, disappointed with what the FBI chose to do with the intel from the raid. To 'avoid panic' they took it upon themselves to keep the entire situation classified. A fancy way to say that they were keeping it a secret from the American people because they unilaterally decided that the public wouldn't be able to handle it.

They decided on sending additional officers across the various agencies to Cartagena to assist in the search for the remaining victims. Regardless of the FBI wanting to keep it under wraps, she had to call Harry and let him know about the update.

Chapter Thirty-Six

Harry and Sharon walked into the police station for a last-minute check-in with Detective Ramos before leaving Panama. Their eyes met across the room, and he smiled and motioned them into his office. "Harry, Sharon, good morning. Another case has been opened in Columbia with an uncanny resemblance to our case. I would like to share the details with you."

"What is it?" asked Sharon, sharing a hopeful look with Harry as they waited for him to explain the connection.

"Two boys were found running on the streets in Columbia, claiming to have been kidnapped from Panama. They were held in a hotel for months and managed to escape of their own volition. Unfortunately, all the kidnapped children and the kidnappers were gone by the time the local police arrived. They have questioned the boys and are currently investigating," Ramos explained.

"What did the boys have to say?" asked Harry, sounding not nearly as desperate as he felt.

"That's why I called you in here, sir. After they were kidnapped, they were taken by boat to Columbia.

As the lead investigator of the Panama abduction cases, Ramos wanted nothing more than to give the parents hope. No. That was not accurate, he noted in his own mind on reflection. What he wanted most of all was to return the child to the parents. His goal in life was to rescue the vulnerable and do all within his power to give them full opportunity to lead a normal life as a family. He did not have children of his own, after very nearly a decade of an otherwise near-perfect marriage. He and his wife, Angeli, had been more excited than either had imagined was possible when she was deemed to be with child. Their child would have been a honeymoon-baby had it survived to full term gestation. But providence had a different fate in mind for the couple. They would endure two more failed pregnancies, and then no more.

Through all those emotionally demanding years and physically taxing losses, Angeli and Bori Ramos had been uplifted by the lyrics penned so many years before by Oscar Hammerstein II.

> *"When you walk through a storm, hold your head up high, and don't be afraid of the dark. At the end of the storm, there's a golden sky, and the sweet silver song of the lark. Walk on through the wind. Walk on through the rain, though your dreams be tossed and blown.*
>
> *Walk on, walk on, with hope in your heart and you'll never walk alone."*

All hope would sadly be wrested from their hearts as Angeli failed to conceive for a fourth time.

It was the Ramos's misfortune to have firsthand knowledge of losing a child. Was it worse to lose a child with whom a bond was only formed in uterus, or a child who had years to form a personality while in your care as a parent? Losing a baby before 24 weeks of pregnancy requires no burial or cremation. This was the situation with the Ramos's first baby. The hospital did however offer the grieving parent a sensitive option to cremate the 18-week-old fetus of their somehow perfectly formed little girl together with the remains of other miscarried babies. The parents, clutching at straws, had seen it as their baby girl's chance to enter the afterlife with the souls of those who had 'suffered' a similar fate. The hospital chaplain had, by way of providing some form on solace, suggested that the baby had in fact not suffered at all.

"Did Christ our Lord not say: Suffer little children to come unto me and forbid them not: for of such is the kingdom of God. Verily I say unto you, whosoever shall not receive the kingdom of God as a little child shall in no wise enter therein."? Those had been his words as he committed the remains of the yet-to-have-lived to whatever it was that awaited them in what may have been eternity. Or may not have been. That was one of the hardest difficulties to face. The not knowing what was in store for their dearly departed. But they chose to hang on to the hope and the promise of paradise.

It did not get easier with each loss. They had been taken to a different hospital when Angeli showed signs of bleeding during her first trimester. Sad to say, the hospital handled the remains of this early loss as clinical waste simply because the distraught parents had not specifically requested otherwise.

The third baby, a son, had been born with a mop of black curls and a distinct cupid's bow. Angeli had delivered him days before he would have been considered typically full term after she had been to see the doctor because she had not felt movement for a day or two. The team in the delivery room, constituting a doctor, the nurses and a midwife had not attempted resuscitation given that the baby had already been dead in utero. So, the little blue boy had been placed on his mother's chest, and the parents given time to say their plaintive goodbyes.

That was the end of their losses. But also, the beginning of their existence as those who would never parent their own biological child. They made the decision not to follow the option of adopting. If Providence deemed them to be childless, then there had to be a valid reason and they would respect their lot in this life.

Detective Bori Ramos would make it his life's mission to ensure that those who had the privilege of being parents, would be reunited with their lost and stolen children. No one should ever feel the weight of losing a child. Not on his watch. His mission was personal and that made it non-debatable.

Chapter Thirty-Seven

Jamie had no idea how long he had slept, but it wasn't long. Sleep had kind of crept up on him and having slept most of the day before certainly hadn't helped. When the men woke him, he was as confused as he usually was after a short nap.

Dan had fallen silent a few hours in, but he still looked tired. Their captors had shaken them awake one by one, handing out bottles of water and ham sandwiches as a breakfast offering.

The majority of the kids in the room had been awoken earlier by the opening of doors and the unnecessarily loud men, but no one appeared to care.

The man spoke quickly, shoving those kids who had finished eating towards the back of the room.

"What's happening?" Jaime asked Dan in a hushed whisper as he was pulled ahead of him.

"It's okay," he replied, looking around to Jaime. "They just want us to take a quick shower and then we'll change into clean clothes."

Jaime scowled, but with enduring the heat, a shower and a fresh set of clothes didn't sound too bad. He was sweating constantly and smelled terrible, and so did the rest of the children around him.

It seemed odd that they had gone to the trouble of kidnapping the children and dragging them out to the middle of nowhere in the heat, just to hand out food and fresh clothing. Nevertheless, having the men shout at him in a language he didn't understand was terrifying. His first instinct was to resist them just because they were forcing him. Seeing Dan going along with what they were doing calmed him somewhat, and he found himself in a group shower similar to those at his school gym.

The cold water was a welcome shock after the all-consuming oppressive heat, and it left Jaime spluttering and shivering in its aftermath. He had no idea how he was going to make it out of here, but the shower and a fresh set of clothes was enough to calm him some.

He was still a little hungry. The sandwich hadn't been enough to fill him. His mother liked to say that a growing boy needed to eat. Her breakfasts were the best. He missed her, not only for the breakfasts, of course, but as his stomach growled loudly, that was certainly what was on his mind. Just bacon, scrambled eggs and buttered toast with jam was all he could think about as he pulled on the new clothes.

Simple clothes were provided; short-sleeved shirts, shorts, socks and shoes. Fresh clean and his exact size. He did have to admit to feeling a little better.

The children were all lined up outside, in the courtyard of the school. The men spoke as if they were expecting someone to arrive.

But after what seemed like hours of standing around during which no one arrived, the men were looking anxious and angry. They snapped at those children who tried to talk to them.

Nobody was coming and they didn't like that. Before the sun reached its peak, they were all lined up and sent back inside. Maybe they were going to be provided with lunch, too.

Chapter Thirty-Eight

Agent Harper stood outside the abandoned school while her team conducted the search. The boys who had escaped had mentioned abandoned schools in the area used to house the children. Having searched three schools, they had yet to make any form of discovery linked to the disappearances. The FBI and the CIA were working together with the Columbian police on this, and they were expecting results not limited to merely charging into the local abandoned schools.

Nothing. A few showed signs of having been lived in, maybe even in the kind of numbers that the boys had indicated, but the apparent residences were now long gone.

"They've been tipped off," Harper said as the agents came out empty handed once again. Two teams were raiding other local schools, but by the looks of it, they weren't having any luck either.

"What makes you say that?" asked Aquino, a member of the Columbian cop contingency.

"They knew that we were going to be raiding the schools," Harper replied, shaking her head. "If it was just the one that the boys escaped from, that would be understandable, but they pulled at least three places clear. That means that someone tipped them off."

"Who?" Aquino asked, shaking his head.

"Well, I don't want to insult your fellow officers around here; I know you're a local..."

Aquino tilted his head. "Where are you from?"

"Born and raised in Florida, but you're a local, right?" Harper countered. "How likely would you say it is that your fellow officers might have let the kidnappers in on our plans?"

Aquino didn't look happy about this line of questioning. His mouth opened, but after a few seconds of thought he paused and snapped it shut again.

"It's a possibility," the officer finally said with a shake of his head. "I mean, sure, corruption is a problem, and them having alerted the kidnappers is possible, but there are some things that you just don't do."

"So, there are acceptable and non-acceptable levels of corruption?" "That's not what I meant, and you know it," Aquino said. "You kind of understand the guys that take a little money on the side to let dealers get away with a bit here and there; that's business. And while it's not acceptable, the guys back at the station don't get too hot under the collar over it. You get to charges of kids being taken, that changes things, you understand?"

Harper nodded. "Well, whether or not it's a possibility for us to look into doesn't really matter. We need to find those kids, and my government has deep pockets, deeper than those of whatever gangs are paying off your officers. So, if you could spread the word around that we'll be grateful to whoever helps us, that would be great."

The officer eyed the agent closely for a few moments before sighing. "I'll see what I can do. For now, though, this place is empty. Let's get out of here."

Chapter Thirty-Nine

The lunch wasn't much more satisfying than the breakfast had been, but it was still better than nothing. More peanut butter and jam sandwiches, more water, and then they were told to take what Dan called a 'siesta'.

"It's what you call it when people take a nap in the afternoon, until it's not so hot anymore," the older boy had said as they all settled into their too-small beds and waited for any sign from the men detaining them.

"They don't let us do anything," Jaime whined as he settled into his bed, crossing his arms rebelliously across his chest. "I'm bored."

Dan shrugged his shoulders. "Maybe they think that we're going to run away. There aren't enough of them to watch us all the time, so if we're always indoors and easy to watch, nobody's running anywhere."

"Still sucks," Jamie complained.

"Yeah, it does," Dan said, leaning back into his bed, shaking his head. "But it could be a lot worse."

"How do you mean?"

Dan didn't answer, raising his hand, moving a little closer to the door where they could hear a couple of the men with raised voices outside. Jaime still couldn't understand whatever language they were speaking, more than likely Spanish, but they sounded angry.

"What are they saying?" Jaime asked, whispering.

"They're talking too quickly," Dan replied, shaking his head and focusing intently. "They're talking about the client. No, the buyer. The buyer is late. Or they aren't coming. And he doesn't like it. They want to talk about staying longer, but they don't want to hang around here any longer."

"Why not?" Jaime asked. "I hate them just pushing us into trucks and driving us all over the place."

"People are looking for us," Dan said. "They don't want to wait around. But they don't want to lose the buyers either. He's talking about how it was difficult to get us all the way down here, and he didn't do it just for the fun of it."

"Don't think anyone's having fun here," Jaime grumbled.

"The buyers are late, so they have to move us out of here," Dan continued, still trying to discern what they were saying. "Anyone that wants to continue can contact them... they're moving us again."

The news was received rather numbly by the rest of the kids, who looked up at the door in response to elevated shouting outside. And then they all heard the sound of the truck being started up again.

"Do you think they'll find us?" Jaime asked.

"I hope so," Dan replied with a small, brave smile.

"Me too!" Jamie said, the excitement bringing a smile to his face.

Chapter Forty

There was not any level of choice of places to eat out here in the middle of nowhere. The officers had nonetheless found themselves here and it wasn't likely they would be moving on to the next spot without at least trying out one of the local street-side restaurants.

Well, restaurant was a little strong, Harper found herself thinking as they arrived at an eatery of sorts place. The appearance suggested that it had been erected by hand without the necessary skills. The majority of the plastic chairs and tables were outside on the porch where patrons could have the benefit of wind and natural air movement, since there was no chance of any form of air conditioning.

The team was able to secure a few seats at the tables, ordering whatever was available that seemed likely to be hot and edible. The local officers were somewhat more trusting, ordering bean stew or chicken with rice. Harper, for her part, was going with whatever was cooked most thoroughly. She ordered a plate of empanadas with a side of the same bean and sausage stew the others were having.

She was hungry, not stupid. As much time as she spent sampling the street food in Miami, Harper doubted that her body was built for the kind of food served hereabouts.

And sure enough, she was hissing as the spicy heat started building in her mouth after only a few forkfuls.

Aquino laughed when he saw the FBI agent red in the face. "They say around here that you can't taste the food unless it's burned into your tongue."

"I actually appreciate the spices," Harper admitted. "Means that the food is preserved."

"Whatever you say, man."

The owner came over to top up their drinks, looking very cautious around the local officers. "Most of the dishes that we serve here are going to be a little hot for the people. But if you prefer, we can get you something that's a little less *caliente*, yes?"

"*Diablos, no,*" Harper said, laughing and then taking a gulp of her drink. "Hot is fine."

"Well, we have some left over from that order we took from those *coños* that came around near closing time last night when we were shutting up," the owner said with a chuckle. "The bastards asked us to cook up a whole bunch of food, and asked for it not to be too spicy, since it was for the *niños*. Who the hell waits until that late to feed their kids?"

Harper blinked a few times before looking up at the man, narrowing her eyes. "Wait, did you deliver to these guys?"

"*Si,* they didn't have the time to wait for us to prepare the food," the owner said. "Gave us directions to a school down the road about fifteen miles and then up the dirt road down to the left."

Harper was almost loathed to believe what she was hearing, looking back to their list of schools in the area. None that the owner had mentioned were in the location.

"Damn it," Harper said, turning to her men. 'Mount up, and fast. There's a school nearby to check. Now, damn it, now!"

The owner looked afraid as they began to rush out while Harper pulled out a few bills to more than cover their orders.

"Thanks for your help, my friend," Harper said, pressing the bills into the man's hand.

"*De nada?*" the owner replied questioningly, but Harper was already headed to a car.

Chapter Forty-One

There were a few places in the world where Harry had never supposed he would end up, even on vacation. North Korea was at the top of the list, but northern South America had always been fairly high too.

Horror stories about what the local drug lords were capable of doing to tourists had always ensured neither he nor his family would ever be found anywhere nearby.

Yet here they were. Finding a small hotel in which to stay just seemed so inconsequential compared with finding their son. In the absence of anything else to do, they weren't going to just stand around waiting for something to happen.

They secured phones that would allow them to stay in touch, but the local law enforcement told them that all they could do was wait by the phone for their call.

Harry wasn't sure why he was surprised to see his phone vibrating almost across the extent of the bedside table.

He pounced on the device before Sharon could, answering it and pressing it to his ear.

"Mr. Giles?" came Harper's familiar voice. Before Harry could reply, she continued, "Just thought that you should know that there has been some intelligence on your son. Children have been reported as being held in a school near to Cartagena. I'll text you the location."

Harry looked down at his phone after Harper had hung up, to see the details of the location she had texted.

"That's not far from here," Sharon said after consulting her laptop. "We can be there in less than half an hour."

Neither thought that it was a good idea to be near a police operation, but they didn't have much of a choice. They got to their rental car and followed the directions which Harry had downloaded on his phone.

They arrived a few minutes after the officers had concluded their sweep. It seemed to have been recently cleared. A pile of dirty clothes had been left behind on the makeshift beds that had been set up for the kids.

"Who are you?" a local officer asked, walking over to the pair. "You cannot be here!"

"That's fine, Aquino, I'll handle them," another responded in perfect English. "Mr. and Mrs. Giles, I presume? We found a few documents that might interest you."

In his extended hand was something which Harry couldn't quite make out in the moment. As his vision cleared, he realized what he was looking at.

"That's my Jaime!" Sharon said loudly. "That's his school ID! Did you find that here?"

The man nodded. "They only left a couple of hours ago, at the most. They couldn't have gotten far, not with the roadblocks that have been set up."

The two returned to their car. They weren't sure what they were going to do but going back to the hotel seemed implausible. They weren't ten minutes down the road before they hit a roadblock.

But it didn't appear to be stopping too many people, who merely detoured, taking advantage of the available side roads.

"What are you doing?" Sharon asked as Harry made to follow suit.

"The roadblock isn't stopping anyone," he replied, not looking back at her. "Let's see where the people that know this place might be heading?"

Chapter Forty-Two

Jamie had learned not to resist the men when they were in a hurry. A couple of the kids had, but they were yelled into submission, cooperating while crying.

The kids were rounded up in a hurry and loaded back into the truck, and it wasn't long before they were on the move yet again.

They started out fast but slowed down abruptly as if they might be caught in traffic. The heat beat down on them mercilessly, crowded into the covered load-body. Jaime could feel sweat soak through his shirt when they finally came to a halt, and a hurried conversation was heard outside.

"Police," Dan whispered to him.

"Can they help us?" Jaime asked, suddenly filled with hope.

That feeling quickly dissipated as he turned back to his friend and saw his dejected look. The conversation outside was a lot less tense than Jaime expected it to be, and after a few minutes they started moving again.

They were moving faster now, and after a minute or so had passed, they were suddenly on a very bumpy road. The driver didn't bother slowing down and hitting the more severe bumps at high speed had caused the kids inside to be tossed around like shuttlecocks.

Jaime was holding on, trying to keep from being thrown off his feet. A couple weren't so lucky, and they were falling about and hitting their heads.

Those who gave in to crying, though, were quickly stopped. One of the men shouted at them, sounding angry and unlikely to be tolerating any more noise from the group. Jaime could see a couple of them reaching for weapons, but none were drawn.

It felt like hours had passed, but it was less than thirty minutes before they stopped again.

Jaime could feel more than a few bruises swelling up from being knocked against the sides of the truck. The men had quickly dismounted, resulting in more conversation between them.

"What are they saying?" Jaime whispered to Dan.

He shrugged. "I can't hear them."

It was pretty faint, but again, they appeared to be talking with a person they knew with whom they were going to be doing business.

The tone of voice was the same as the one Jaime's father used when he was talking to a business associate. Kind of fake, and yet the effort that was put into faking it made it sound real.

They didn't talk for long, and finally the truck started moving again after only a few minutes. The road was still bumpy, but the going was slower this time.

Once they came to a halt, the men started shouting and indicating for the children to move off. Jaime looked around, seeing that they were in what looked like an old barn.

"Where are we?" he asked, still whispering.

"Somewhere that the police won't find us," Dan said, looking like he was struggling with maintaining his impossible optimism.

Chapter Forty-Three

"What are you watching?" Harry asked, stepping out of the shower.

Sharon looked around at him. "Oh, they're talking about a police operation in a hotel on the other side of Cartagena. They found a group of kidnapped kids being held there and arrested a group of the kidnappers."

"Wait, what?" Harry asked. "Since when do you speak Spanish?"

"Since never, I got a call from Harper while you were in the shower," Sharon said, her voice in a low monotone.

He didn't need to question her mood. He'd seen this coping mechanism in the past.

"I guess… Jaime…"

"He wasn't with the kids they recovered," Sharon said, her voice trembling slightly. "I… well, it's nice, since quite a few parents are now reunited with their children."

Harry tried to smile, but it was a struggle. Sure, he could be happy for the families that had been and would still be reunited, but their Jaime was still missing and out there, somewhere, all alone and scared.

"They're going to find him, sweetie," Harry said, hugging his wife closely. She hugged him back, and a few seconds later he could feel her sobbing into his chest. "They're going to find him."

Chapter Forty-Four

The longer they stayed in that barn, the tenser the situation appeared between the men who were their captors. Not one appeared to be willing to leave, but it wasn't long before they showed signs of needing more than just the shelter that that barn provided.

Food and water became an issue between the men during the two days that they were to spend in the barn until they were finally willing to move again. Jaime couldn't remember being this hungry ever in the past, but he moved with the rest of the kids, trying to keep his spirits up.

It was difficult, but not impossible.

Back in the truck, they only moved at night until they reached what looked like a small compound buried deep in the nearby mountains.

An abundance of food and water was available here, and they were all treated to a welcome hot meal, followed shortly after by showers and another change of clothes. Those that they had worn during their extended time inside the barn had quickly become ragged.

The group of men looked a little calmer and a lot more relaxed. It was a relief to have sufficient food and water supplies, but the children were still restless, unsure as to what would be happening next.

Once they were finished dressing in their new clothes, they could hear a car pulling up near the building that served as their makeshift prison. Jaime craned his neck to see a tall, dark-skinned man coming over and talking to their captors, shaking their hands and patting them on the side of the head, in a way that made it seem that he was comforting them.

It took him a few minutes to find his way to their group, smiling broadly and showing a perfect set of pure white teeth.

"Good evening, children. How are you all tonight?" he asked in perfect English.

There was no response. Jaime had no idea just how they were expected to respond in this situation.

"Alright then," the man continued as if he hadn't been expecting an answer anyway. "My name is Sam, and I'm here to make sure that you're all very, very comfortable. Things might seem a little confusing now, but don't you worry about a thing. It won't be long before you all get set up with your new families. Families who will love you very much. You might miss your mommies and daddies now, but soon you'll be rich, and forget all about them, okay? Now get some sleep."

Sam turned and walked away, and the guards guided them towards the beds that they would be spending the night in.

"At least we have real beds this time," Dan said, settling into the cot next to Jaime's.

Jaime didn't answer, curling up on the clean sheets as the lights went out. He didn't know what they were talking about. He didn't want a new family, rich or otherwise. He wanted his own.

He couldn't help the few tears that escaped his eyes, running slowly down his cheeks to drop onto his pillow. More came. Sobs wracked his chest even as he could feel himself drifting off, dreaming of home.

Part Two

Far from Home

Chapter One

JAMIE SHOT OUT OF BED, his heart pounding in his chest. He could sense a light sheen of sweat on his skin and his sheets felt damp. He had had a nightmare and the feeling of someone hunting and tracking him down, but the longer that he was awake, the more the dream faded from his mind, leaving only the memory of a feeling.

He pushed himself over the edge of the bed, yawning and rubbing some feeling into his eyes. Just a quick trip down to the kitchen for a glass of water, and he would be fine.

Jamie looked up from where he was sitting on his bed, seeing rows and rows of other beds around him, where dozens of children were currently sleeping.

He remembered that there was no downstairs. He sighed. A few days ago, the realization would have been enough to make him cry, but that feeling had also faded. Crying wasn't going to get him anywhere and wanting to be home would do even less.

All he could do was wait, just like all the other kids.

Jamie settled back into his bed, looking up to see lights shining through the cracks of the wooden walls around them. He pushed himself up to the slats to look through them. It took his eyes a few seconds to adjust, but he could see and hear a truck pulling up outside, the same way that they had been brought in.

More or less the same time too, he noted. They'd spent a few days inside a barn, and were then driven up further into the mountains in the dead of night. The kidnappers hadn't let them stay anywhere for too long, driving them all over the country in that truck of theirs. And the country, he reminded himself, wasn't the United States, it was Columbia.

The truck that was outside even looked like the same one he had arrived in, he thought, looking around. None of the other kids were woken up by the noise, oddly enough. Maybe they were just too tired.

Jamie peeked through the slats again, seeing the men outside using flashlights as the truck found a place to park. Jamie narrowed his eyes as he watched the men shouting, and children jumping out of the back and being herded towards one of the other buildings that had been used as their hideout for the past week or so.

It was better than the barn that they had slept in for two days, as well as the school, if he was honest. The kids had been sleeping on mats on the floor at the school, but at least here they had beds, and an actual kitchen. Before arriving here, they had been surviving on whatever food could be picked up nearby.

He wasn't going to say that it was the best situation that he'd ever been in, but he would take the improvements. And it certainly beat being on a stinking, loud truck on a bumpy road. Or the boat or submarine he had been on before that, which had both made him seasick.

More kids were being brought in. Jamie had no idea how they were finding those kids, or how they'd found him. He wondered if they would be crying themselves to sleep for their first day here too.

Jamie settled back into his bed, looking up at the roof above him and tried to go back to sleep.

Chapter Two

SLEEP DIDN'T COME. It wasn't like he needed to wake up early for school tomorrow, but, as he had learned recently, he felt bad all day if he didn't sleep much (or at all, as was often the case). He kept staring up at the roof until he could see little spears of light cutting through the cracks in the walls, illuminating the dark building that they were in.

He heard a door close and looked to see who had come in. While remaining still, he watched as a pair of men came into the room where they were sleeping, moving quickly and quietly, unlike whenever they were moving the kids and wanted to make sure that they could be seen and heard.

The sneaky nature of their movements was what grabbed Jamie's attention, especially in this case. They had papers in their hands, and whispered a bit between each other, and immediately made their way to two of the other beds.

One of which was Dan's bed. Even though he was one of the bigger kids there, he was still lifted up from the bed, almost without effort, and a hand was placed firmly over his mouth to muffle any noise that he might make.

Another one of the other older boys was picked up, and both were quickly taken out of the room. Jamie then heard a car start up and drive away.

Only after the sound of the car had faded did Jamie realize that he was holding his breath. Where were his friends being taken now? Was he going to be taken next?

A few minutes passed before the door opened up again, and Sam stepped inside, turning the lights on.

"Good morning, everyone!" Sam called. "Let's get on up! Breakfast is ready and waiting, and you need to get on up and get it before it runs out!"

He'd said the same thing every time they were woken up, and never had the food ever been at risk of running out. But it never failed to get them all up. Nobody wanted to be left without any food.

Jamie got up from his bed, stretching and yawning. He still felt stiff despite the fact that he had been awake for hours. He moved over to the door where Sam was ushering them through.

"Mr. Sam?" Jamie asked as he approached the man.

"Just Sam, please," he replied, smiling and turning to Jamie. "Jamie, right? What's up?"

"It's just…" Jamie hesitated. "I saw that they took some kids earlier this morning. One of them-Dan, he's my best friend."

"Oh, don't worry about them, Jamie," Sam said, lowering himself to his haunches to be at Jamie's eye level. "I can't tell you where they are right now, but you can trust me when I tell you that they are safe. Safer than ever, actually."

Jamie wasn't sure why he trusted the man that was talking to him, but there was something about the man's dark eyes that made Jamie want to believe that what he was saying was true. Besides, it only made sense that he was telling the truth. They wouldn't have gone to all of the trouble to bring all the kids this far only to hurt them or put them in danger.

They all headed towards the "mess hall," which was another building like the one where Jamie slept, but instead of beds there were long wooden tables and stools. They had been eating their meals here since they had arrived.

Jamie saw another group of kids was already here. These must be the kids that had arrived late last night, he thought. They looked to be what he considered ordinary kids, American like himself. These kids were about his age and younger, not like the others already here who were mostly older than him. They looked tired and dirty, much like he had been after riding in the back of a truck for days. The new kids had already piled their plates full of rice porridge and buttered toast that had been prepared for them.

Jamie grabbed his own plate and joined them, sitting across from a group of children who were trying to figure out where they were.

"I'm Jamie," he said, looking around at the new kids.

They introduced themselves one by one around the table. Most of them looked to be American.

"Mark."

"Jenny."

"Tom."

"Sherry."

Jamie nodded, looking around to the rest of them. "I'm from Massachusetts."

"San Francisco, California," said Mark.

"Berkley, California too," said Jenny.

"Seattle," said Tom.

"Vancouver, BC" said Sherry.

There were a few younger kids that didn't say anything.

Jamie looked at Sherry for a moment and scrunched his face, trying to remember where Vancouver was. He'd been a little fuzzy on geography.

Sherry noticed his confusion and helped him out. "I'm from Canada."

"Oh, right," Jamie said, shaking his head. Of course, Canada. "You're all off of the West Coast, right? Me and the other kids here are from the East Coast. They picked us up a couple of weeks ago... I... I don't remember much, they kept me asleep for most of the time. I think they picked me up from my school playground and drove me out. Then I was on a boat, and I think a submarine too. They were taking a bunch of us out here."

"Where is out here?" Sherry asked.

"Somewhere in South or Latin America, I think," Mark chimed in. "They're all speaking Spanish and the heat too."

"They had us on a boat for most of the way," Tommy said. "And then in a truck for almost a week. Only let us out to use the bathroom."

"You're lucky," Jamie pointed out. "We couldn't even stop for bathroom breaks on the submarine. No windows, all just cramped."

"Hey, I remember that," Tom said. "There was a little bathroom on board. I thought it was a dream though."

They all nodded and a few of the younger children giggled and whispered at the bathroom talk. They all looked a little scared and terrified over their situation. Maybe seeing the other kids that were there with them calmed them down a bit. It was good, Jamie thought. It wasn't good that they were here but being calm was going to be in their best interests.

Jamie dug in and the new kids followed suit. They were in it together now.

Chapter Three

DAN CAME BACK later that night in time for dinner, but not the other boy. He looked a little subdued when he settled in next to them.

"What happened to the other boy?" Jamie asked in a hushed whisper.

"He got sold," Dan replied. "These rich people bought him with a bag full of money."

"What about you?" Jamie asked.

"They only wanted one," Dan said. "They liked him better, I guess. The guards asked if they wanted both of us but they only took him," Dan said.

It was hard not to think about. Being sold off to rich strangers had seemed like such a perfect idea when Sam talked about it, but seeing the look in Dan's eyes, it was difficult for him to shake a bad feeling about it.

Sleeping wasn't an option again that night, even though he hadn't gotten much of it the night before.

It didn't really matter. Sleep came the next night, and then the night after that. A few more weeks of sleep, and the days started merging together. It was wake up, eat, do some exercise, lunch, chores, dinner, free time and then bed. It was a boring schedule, but Jamie was able to get to know his new friends; Mark, Jenny, Tom and Sherry.

Dan got in with them eventually too. It was difficult not to be friends with them since they were all living together now, but it took Dan a little longer because he was older.

Most of the guards left them alone except when they gave the kids orders; the only one to harass them was Marco. Marco gave them grief if they were talking when they were meant to be exercising or doing chores, which reminded Jamie of teachers in school. He also called the kids names in Spanish sometimes. Jamie didn't understand at first but Dan sometimes translated for him. Marco called Tom, who was chubby, pig-boy, and he called Jenny a chicken, which Jamie didn't really get.

Marco never bothered them when Sam was around though. Sam was nice. He was always willing to answer any of their questions and he made sure that they had everything they needed. Jamie found himself liking and trusting the tall, lean dark-skinned man, as he seemed to have their safety at heart.

***

JAMIE HAD ALMOST FORGOTTEN about Dan's little trip until late one night when he woke up to guards in the sleeping quarters in the middle of the night again. Sam was with them this time. The guards had their lists in hand again and started picking the children up.

Jamie couldn't believe that he was the only one that was awake for this. One of the men moved over his bed which made Jamie cover his mouth. His heart pounded in his chest. Then there was a whispered command from the other side of the room.

The man standing over his bed stopped, turning to see Sam shaking his head.

Three more boys were taken out of the building. The three men that took them returned but not the boys.

***

SLEEPING BECAME DIFFICULT again. Jamie got another chance to talk to Sam alone the next day.

"Sam," Jamie said. "What happened to the three kids that left yesterday?"

"Don't worry, they are safe," Sam said. He looked at Jamie's face and knew that he wasn't satisfied with this answer. He sighed and looked around to make sure they were alone.

"Look, I'm not supposed to tell you this, so it's just between the two of us, okay?" When Jamie nodded, Sam continued, looking away. "There are some bad people, who are really powerful. They were after your parents as well as the parents of all the other kids that are here. I don't know why, but they knew something they shouldn't have known, and the bad guys wanted to kill them all."

"What bad people?" Jamie asked, eyes wide. "Are my mom and dad okay?"

"I don't know," Sam said, looking Jamie in the face, and then looking away again. "We didn't wait to see. My partner, Diego, and I saved you and most of the other kids. We had to get you out of the country because the bad men had friends in the FBI."

Jamie just looked at him, tears streaming down his face. Sam took his hand.

"I know this is hard to hear, but we're trying to find new homes for you, somewhere you'll be safe, and the bad men will never get you. We can't stay here forever. Those boys we took yesterday, all three of them were adopted. Rich people that couldn't have children adopted them, so don't worry. They're living better than they ever did."

It sounded like a fairy tale. Dad had always said that when something sounded too good to be true, it usually was. But he trusted Sam. He had to. Sam was the only one who seemed to care about them and the only one to tell them anything.

Jamie was overwhelmed with grief and fear, knowing that his parents were probably dead. Sam led him back to his bed and sat next to him until Jamie drifted off to sleep.

Chapter Four

MORE NIGHTS of difficult sleep followed. The rest of the kids seemed to understand the situation and they were handling it better than he was. Most of the other kids, anyway.

"Jamie, are you awake?"

He turned to see Dan standing over his bed.

"Yeah."

"Come on," Dan said, leading Jamie over to the other side of the building.

Jamie could hear voices shouting outside the building as some headlights were shining through the cracks. Dan didn't need to tell him to get down low and listen.

"...paying money to keep them fed, and I'm not getting anything back!" said a voice that they didn't recognize. They were speaking in Spanish, but Jamie was starting to learn the language and by now he could make out bits and pieces.

"We're working on it," Sam said, also in Spanish. He sounded a lot calmer than the other man. "They're being handled, but we couldn't move them any faster, thanks to the heat that was brought down on the operation."

"I don't care," the man replied, clearly the one in charge. "Move them faster. Get them out of here. I need to make my money back to start another project. Move them to the city if you have to."

"No, we don't need to move them to the city," Sam said quickly. "Anything but that. I'll work on moving them faster and contacting more clients."

"See that you do," the man snarled. "You're in charge here because I put you in charge. That can change anytime that I say."

"I understand," Sam said.

Dan and Jamie pulled away from the wall.

"Did you understand that?" Dan asked.

Jamie nodded. "Most of it. I think I'm getting the hang of Spanish."

"Good, you'll need it," Dan said, sitting on the floor. Jamie dropped down next to him.

"Why?" Jamie asked.

Dan shrugged. "I might not be around for much longer to translate for you. You might not be around for much longer either."

"Come on, don't talk like that." Jamie said. He knew what Dan was getting at, but he was afraid to voice the words.

"Why not?" Dan asked. "We know what's going to happen to us here. We're not going to live here forever. They're going to 'move' us sooner or later."

"Don't think about that," Jamie said, placing a hand on his shoulder. "For now, we're together. And that's all that matters."

Chapter Five

"BOSS!" Marco shouted. "someone's coming!"

Jamie and Dan looked up from the outside exercise area, looking over to where Marco was calling out to Sam.

Sam looked around from where he was working, and to see what Marco was calling him about.

It took them a few seconds to see what the commotion was about. More of the men were starting to move in, shouting at the kids to run, and gesturing towards the trees.

A clearly marked police car with flashing lights on top was approaching the entrance.

"Get them out of sight," Sam said in Spanish. The men were already doing that, pushing the kids out of sight back behind the trees.

"You think we can use this?" Dan asked as he and Jamie ducked down behind some bushes together.

"What do you mean?" Jamie asked.

"They're all distracted," Dan said, looking around. He wasn't wrong, as most of the men were focused on the car that was pulling up to the entrance. Not on the kids, at least not after they were put out of sight.

"And go where?" Jamie asked. "We're in the middle of the jungle here."

"Go to the cop," Dan said. "Tell him what's happening, and then let him take us back to his station or something. Come on!"

Dan moved out from behind the bush, indicating for Jamie to follow him, but he couldn't. He wasn't sure why but moving out in the open like this... he just couldn't.

Marco looked over to see Dan out in the open, and reached for his pocket. Jamie had seen him pull a pistol from that pocket before, but he didn't say anything.

Sam was walking over to where the gate was opening, and a man in uniform was walking up. If they were going to make it out, it was now.

Dan paused in his step, not moving when he saw Sam pulling an envelope from his pocket and putting it into the hands of the uniformed man, who laughed, waved and put on a pair of sunglasses before returning to his car. A minute passed before he turned the car around and headed away.

The police weren't going to help them. When Dan moved back behind the bushes Jamie came to the same realization as he did.

Marco's hand moved away from his pocket.

Chapter Six

JAMIE WASN'T SURE if it was the police visit that triggered it, or if Sam was just delivering on his promises to 'move' the children quicker, but more children were disappearing from the building every night.

None of those that left were coming back; they were being 'moved', whatever that meant. Sam insisted that they were all going to rich families who were going to be taking better care of them than their own families had.

Jamie still found no reason to not trust what Sam was saying. They were there for a reason, after all. But it still felt wrong, somehow. The visit from the police had put all the men on edge. The day after the visit, Jamie heard Marco shouting at Sam in Spanish, but faster than Jamie was able to understand, and using many words that he didn't understand.

***

THE BOSS CAME around again a few days later, talking to Sam while Dan and Jamie listened in. It was always the same; the kids needed to be moved faster. More projects coming up. Jamie wondered if the "projects" involved more kids.

Jamie finally managed to sleep well for a few nights, but he shouldn't have. It wasn't that he didn't need the sleep, but when he woke up, he realized that

Dan's bed was empty. Jamie had been sleeping too deeply to have heard anyone coming in for him.

It was usually three or four kids that disappeared at a time. One being gone either meant that he was picked out specifically, or because he hadn't been picked at all.

No, Dan wouldn't have left without telling him. And not without causing a ruckus with the guards. They were all quiet while escorting the kids over to the mess hall for breakfast. Even quieter than usual. Marco was also gone, so he must be with Dan.

"What happened to Dan?" Jamie asked Sam when no one was in earshot. "Did he get adopted?"

"No, nothing like that," Sam said, shaking his head.

"Is he okay?" Jamie asked.

"He should be fine, Jamie," Sam said, patting Jamie on the shoulder. "Just head on in and get yourself some breakfast, okay? Don't worry about it."

Don't worry about it. That was excellent advice. He trusted Sam, but there was no way that he wasn't going to worry about Dan. He wished he could help. He wished he could do something. Anything.

Chapter Seven

AS IT TURNED OUT, a whole day of not worrying about it was impossible. He couldn't bring himself to talk or play with Sherry, Tom, or any of the others. They were missing Dan too, but it bugged Jamie the most. Dan was his best friend. Or he had been anyway.

Jamie wasn't sure how he was going to make it without Dan there with him. He didn't even want to think about it, and the only thing Sam said, other than not to worry about it, was that he hadn't been adopted.

Another sleepless night followed. Jamie wasn't sure how he was going to survive like this, tossing and turning in bed, just thinking about what had happened to Dan, and what was going to happen to him. Time crawled until he could see the first rays of sunlight through the slats.

Then the door opened and Sam came in, showing Dan back to his bed.

Jamie jumped up to his feet, running over to them. Dan looked tired, more than tired; he looked like he had just been through three hours of gym.

And, impossible though it seemed, Sam looked worse. The man had always looked pristine and elegant, but he looked disheveled now. Tired and even more exhausted than Dan looked.

Sam left without saying a word, and Dan dropped down on his bed, shaking his head.

"What happened?" Jamie asked once Sam was gone.

"I don't want to talk about it," Dan replied.

Jamie placed a hand on Dan's shoulder as he looked up at the roof, not saying a word.

"It was Marco," Dan finally said, closing his eyes. "He grabbed me in the middle of the night. I think he heard that I wanted to try escape, and he wanted to make an example. He said that he wanted to wake up all the kids to make them watch while he hurt me. He was distracted for a second, and I got away from him. I don't know how, but I got out to the jungle and hid."

"Why didn't you run away?" Jamie asked, squeezing Dan's shoulder. He wasn't sure what else to say or do other than help his friend. It had been a long night for Jamie, and he could only imagine the kind of night Dan had.

"It's like you said," he replied, closing his eyes. "We're in the middle of the jungle. Where could I run to?"

It was an odd thing to think about. They were out in the middle of the jungle with nowhere to escape, even if they wanted to. And Jamie wasn't even sure if he wanted to run away. He wanted to go home, but he wasn't going to do that alone.

"Did they hurt you?" Jamie asked. "When they found you, I mean?"

"No, Sam told Marco off and brought me here himself," Dan said. "He didn't want Marco to hurt me."

There were a hundred different questions that Jamie wanted to ask, but Dan looked like he hadn't had any sleep-in days. He probably hadn't, and his eyes were drifting shut.

"Get some sleep," Jamie said, and Dan didn't have anything to say back. He was already falling asleep, eyes shut and settled back in his bed.

Jamie would get his answers after Dan had gotten his rest. He patted his friend on the shoulder and headed back to his own bed.

Chapter Eight

DAN needed most of the day to recover from his ordeal. Jamie still wasn't sure why it was that he had been brought back by Sam. They didn't appear to have much tolerance for the kids trying to run away, but at this point, he wasn't going to be asking any questions. Seeing the way that Marco was glaring at him and Sam was enough to make Jamie want to keep his head down.

No need for any more trouble at this point.

It was a long day, and after a while, Jamie almost didn't care about the glares that he was getting from Marco.

When dinner time arrived, the kids were all herded into the mess hall, and when Jamie looked up, he was surprised to see that Dan had joined them. He looked tired, like he had just woken up.

Jamie could only imagine that his friend needed at least another night of rest.

The most surprising, of course, was that Sam was with him. The taller man was guiding Dan to one of the tables, speaking softly in his ear before directing him towards one of the seats.

Marco was unhappy. That much was obvious from the way he immediately approached Sam and Dan. Sam quickly stepped in front of Marco.

Marco was saying something quickly and angrily. Jamie wasn't able to pick up on every detail, but he could hear a few words that he recognized. One in particular was repeated often; 'culpa' was a word that Jamie had heard before, usually meaning guilt.

From the way that Marco was poking his finger into Sam's chest and trying to intimidate him, Jamie could guess that Marco was blaming Dan's running away on Sam. Jamie wasn't sure why.

Sam stared the man down, barely moving and not reacting as Marco tried to push back at him.

"It's your fault!" Marco said loudly. "I tried to teach him a lesson."

Sam's expression changed and he didn't answer immediately. When he did, it wasn't with words. Jamie could see it coming a moment before, just watching the way that Sam's hand came up, faster than he could blink. Sam connected his fist with Marco's jaw hard enough to spin the man around and send him to the ground.

"*Hijo de...*" Marco started to say, but Sam stepped in and kicked him in the stomach.

Marco groaned, curling up on the ground, clutching his stomach.

After a second, he turned around and threw up on the ground. Jamie made a face, as did most of the kids present.

"Get him up," Sam said to one of the other guards. "Get him to one of the cars."

Jamie wasn't sure where they were going but he was relieved that Marco was gone. Sam would take care of things, he knew.

Jamie picked up his plate, and moved over to where Dan was sitting. Dan still didn't look like he was willing to talk, and that was alright. Jamie was just going to sit with him for a while, in silence, if need be.

Sam got back about an hour later. They had just finished with their dinner. He walked with a bit of a limp, and Jamie thought that he could see some red splotches on his blue shirt which he hadn't noticed before they left.

Marco wasn't with him when they returned, Jamie noted as he headed back to the building where they were going to spend the night.

"I guess Marco's gone," Dan said, keeping his head low.

He was right. They never saw Marco again.

Chapter Nine

THERE WEREN'T MANY KIDS left. The boss, who Jamie heard Sam call "Diego," was telling Sam to 'move' the kids quicker, and that was what they were doing.

There weren't as many guards now either. Marco was gone and Diego had taken one of the others with him to do "Another job."

Or, at least, that was what Sam had said when he said that they were all moving to the next building.

It wasn't going to be difficult. The building that they had been in wasn't exactly home, and the new one had fewer holes in the walls, and in the ceiling. It hadn't rained during their time there yet, but Jamie had a feeling that was going to change. He didn't know much about this place, but he knew what a rainforest looked like, and the fact that they usually dealt with rain.

Once they were finished moving, Jamie turned to see Sam standing at the door, looking at him and Dan.

"I'm going to need the two of you to follow me now, please," Sam said softly, indicating with his head. "We're going for a ride."

"The same kind of ride that you took with Marco?" Dan asked.

Jamie looked around, fearful of Sam's reaction, but all he could see on the man's face was a small smile. "No, nothing like that kind of ride."

Dan and Jamie looked at each other. There was no point in resisting, and they quickly joined Sam in a car. Another guard was already behind the wheel.

"We've found a family," Sam explained once they were out of the compound. "They're rich and happy, but they want a pair of boys to enrich their lives, and they would be more than happy to take the two of you in and give you a home."

Jamie looked over to Dan, tilting his head. Once more, it seemed that they had little choice in the matter, but they were going to meet people they knew nothing about. He hoped Sam was right and they were good people.

They pulled out in front of what looked like a small abandoned building, still in the middle of the rainforest. They didn't have much time, and Jamie found himself and Dan being quickly pulled out of the vehicle as another vehicle pulled in next to them.

A tall man with a bald head and wearing a suit stepped out of the other car, pulling off a pair of sunglasses.

"What happened here?" he asked in an accent that Jamie didn't recognize.

"We were told that you were looking for a pair of boys," Sam said. "These two are almost as close as brothers."

"I'm sorry, there must have been some kind of misunderstanding," the man said, shaking his head. "My wife and I are only looking for one son. One that we won't have to raise. The older one will do." He handed Sam an envelope which Sam opened, removing the money and quickly counting it before nodding at the other guard.

The driver quickly grabbed Dan by the arms, and took him to the car.

"Wait!" Jamie pleaded, and Sam stopped him by placing a hand on his shoulder. "What are they doing?"

"Daniel has a new home now," Sam said in a soft voice as Jamie fought back tears. "With parents that will love him and provide him with everything he'll ever need or want. I was hoping they would take you too, but it didn't work out. Don't worry; we're going to find you a new home soon, okay?"

Jamie felt numb as he walked back to the car. Sam seemed to think that he was crying because he wasn't getting a home himself, and not because his best friend was being taken away, likely never to return.

Jamie hid his face as the car started again, pressing it into the seat and not wanting to look at the other car pulling away. He hadn't even had the chance to say goodbye.

His chest hurt as the sobs were wrenched out. They pulled away from where they had parked, and headed back to the compound.

Chapter Ten

JAMIE HAD FALLEN ASLEEP. The last thing he remembered was crying into his pillow as the lights were turned off for the night. But shortly after they were turned back on again.

Sam was rushing in, looking worried as he passed on some instructions in Spanish to one of the other guards, who was waking the remaining five children that hadn't been 'moved'.

It was just the two guards, it seemed, and while they were keeping their voices down, Jamie could see the urgency in their expressions.

They needed to move, and fast.

It wasn't like they had any possessions to gather before heading out, and it wasn't that long before the group was heading out of the building, and as it turned out, out of the compound entirely into the trees.

Jamie rubbed his eyes and yawed as they moved into the forest. He could see that Sam had a flashlight in his hand, but he hadn't turned it on yet.

The tall man paused, looking back down to the compound that they had just left, and Jamie did the same.

He suddenly realized why they had left so quickly.

The place had been swarmed by a group of cars with bright flashing lights. The police appeared to be raiding the place, and while they were already a good distance away, he could see that a handful of the guards were being rounded up and put down on their stomachs with their hands behind their backs.

"Americano," the other guard said to Sam as they continued to move.

"Good thing we got away," Sam replied in Spanish, and Jamie could only just understand him. "Can't buy those guys. We had ten minutes of warning, so we should be counting our lucky stars."

"What about the guys that we left behind?" the second man asked, nudging one of the children that was starting to lag.

"Most of them are wanted for other things," Sam replied. "They kept the cops busy long enough for us to get away."

Jamie shook his head, trying to stay focused on navigating through the darkness. Sure, he didn't doubt that the officers would arrest the guards, but if that was all they managed to do, how was that going to help him and the other children?

Were they going to start looking through the forest for them? Were the guards that got themselves arrested going to inform the cops where they were likely to end up?

Jamie doubted both of these. They needed to focus on getting through the rainforest without getting lost. He wondered if there were any lions or snakes or anything like that. One thing was for sure, he was glad that Sam was with them.

Jamie fought the impulse to start crying again and he quickly brushed his forearms across his cheeks to wipe away those tears of fear that escaped. He tried to clear the tears in his eyes; it was hard enough to see in the dark as it was.

Chapter Eleven

SAM wasn't sure how things had gotten so bad.

Sure, the life that he was living, one that was forced upon him, tended to get messy sometimes. But he liked to think that he'd made the best of one hell of a bad situation.

But there had always been the possibility that things were going to end up going to hell.

Sure, they had already had some trouble with this work. Nobody had known how close the US authorities had gotten so fast, or for the Colombian authorities to be cooperating with them.

Sam really hadn't expected himself to start connecting with these children the way that he had. It was hard not to see himself in them. The darkness of his own childhood had come up in a roaring mess to defend them in any way he could.

But he was still there to do a job, which included keeping them away from the local police, the honest ones that weren't going to get bought off.

They had been up in the forest for almost a full week, and things had gone from bad to worse. The kids were tired and had been walking without water or food. Jamie was the first one to succumb; two days ago, he'd started developing a fever, and started throwing up the next. It wasn't long before he passed out and wouldn't wake up.

He only got worse from that point on. He needed medical attention, but they were too far from civilization to find a hospital, even if they wanted to.

Ramiro had already gone off to find some source of food or water when the children fell asleep, leaving Sam to keep an eye on them.

But Jamie was the one that he found himself watching over, checking his temperature from time to time and replacing the wet towel on his forehead. Sam had spent most of the day carrying Jamie, and while he could feel the aches and pains, he almost couldn't feel them.

All he wanted was for the child to feel better, somehow.

"I'm so sorry," Sam said softly, shaking his head. "I'm sorry we got you all the way out here in the middle of nowhere. I wish you could have just ended up with that family, or maybe back with your own family. I bet they were great for you. Maybe not perfect, but they tried their best to give you a good life."

It was weird how that was the thought that came to his mind. Thinking about the family that Jamie had come from almost allowed him to put himself in that position, imagining what it would have been like to have a family to call his own.

Sam shook his head, wiping a couple of tears that had escaped. He just wished that Jamie would get better.

He let out a deep, shaky sigh, settling back against a nearby tree and tried to think about something else.

Chapter Twelve

JAMIE realized that he'd fallen asleep. It was hard to shake the fact that they had all had a long week and needed the sleep.

Besides, all the children were still there, and none of them had even woken up yet.

They had been through a long few days as well.

Sam pushed himself up, stretching and rolling his shoulders before checking what few supplies that they had managed to pick up from the compound before deserting it.

It had mostly been bottled water and what little food he could grab, as well as some flashlights, batteries and water purifying tablets.

He would have thought that being in a rain forest there would be a bit more water readily available to them. Ramiro had been gone for a while, almost the whole night, and if Sam had to guess, the guy had just decided to cut it and run.

Then again, he knew better than to turn against their employer. That is probably why the guards that had been caught by the cops wouldn't pose a problem to the man. Everybody in the country knew better.

Less than an hour after the sun started to rise, when the children started to wake up, Jamie could hear footsteps of the man returning. He tried to open his eyes but he couldn't

"How did your search go?" Sam asked.

"What, no good morning?" Ramiro asked, looking tired and annoyed. "How have you been?"

"Good morning, how have you been?" Sam asked, rolling his eyes. "How did your search go?"

The man sighed, rubbing his eyes gently. "I found some running water a few kilometers to the east. How's the sick kid? What's his name again?"

"Jamie," Sam replied, moving over to the pale and sickly-looking child, placing a hand on his forehead. "Looks like his fever broke during the night. Getting him some food and water would do him well, though."

"I don't know where the food will come from, but I guess we can figure that out later," Ramiro replied as they roused the rest of the children, spreading the last of their food out among them for breakfast before starting out and heading towards the river that Ramiro had mentioned.

Sam found himself carrying Jamie in his arms yet again, but he didn't really begrudge the responsibility. It wasn't like Jamie was that heavy anyway. He was a small kid, even for his age, and being sick certainly hadn't helped.

"Just stay with us, little buddy," Sam found himself saying with every little bump that could have woken up Jamie. He appeared to still be unconscious, but he looked better than he was the night before, when Sam was worrying for his life.

Jamie's eyes opened and the boy moaned just as they arrived at the edge of what looked like a broad, yet very shallow river that was cutting through the forest like a knife.

"Morning," Sam said, settling him down on the ground. "How are you feeling?"

"My head hurts," Jamie said with the honesty of a child. "And I'm thirsty. Really thirsty."

"Well, lucky for you, we've got a whole river of water to drink," Sam said, getting an empty water bottle from his backpack and bending down to fill it from the stream He handed it to Jamie.

He went through the water quickly, and Sam quickly replaced his suddenly empty bottle with another full one.

"Take it easy now," Sam said softly. You drink too much you'll throw up.

"*Oye!*" came a voice from the forest behind them.

Sam and Ramiro both froze in place.

"*Manos arriba, ahora!*" shouted the voice again, and both of them complied with the request, raising their hands and turning around to see a man with a shotgun pointed at their heads.

Chapter Thirteen

SAM HAD BEEN REGRETTING the fact that they hadn't had the time to collect the weapons that they had stashed at the compound for a few days now. Before it had been because having a gun would make hunting for food a lot easier.

But as of right now, all he could think was that it would be nice to be able to shoot back if things went sour.

At least the children were smart enough to remain absolutely still while staring wide-eyed at the man that was coming down from the woods, his weapon still pointed steadily at them.

At least he wasn't a cop, that much was certain. And it didn't appear as though he had anyone with him.

"What are you doing here?" the man asked in the rough Spanish that they spoke in these parts. "Who are you? Why are you trespassing on my land?"

"I'm sorry," Sam said, keeping his hands raised. "We were a part of a tour group that was caught in a firefight between the police and the cartels. We had to abandon our bus and run, and we got lost in the forest. We didn't mean to intrude on your land."

Sam knew how to be a good liar when he wanted to be. It had been a matter of survival for him. Even so, the man, who looked to be a farmer, didn't look completely convinced. Even so, the sight of the hungry-looking children was enough to make him lower the weapon.

"How long have you been out here for?" the man asked.

"About a week now," Sam replied, honestly.

"*Dios mio*, are you insane?" the man asked, shaking his head. "These forests are no place for children. You'll die of malaria or get eaten by a panther or something. Come along now, my farm is not that far away. We can get you all some food."

"Thank you, thank you so much," Sam said, indicating for the children to follow him as he followed the farmer himself. "I don't know if you have some kind of phone that we could use to contact the school? We need to let the parents know that their children are alright."

"Sure, I have a phone here," the man said. Sam could tell that he still wasn't convinced that Sam was who he said he was. Honestly, he didn't blame him. Sam looked like he could have been a teacher, but Ramiro had cartel hit man written all over him.

Sam punched in the number that he had memorized a long time ago, letting it ring for a few seconds before someone picked up.

"Hello?" came Diego's voice.

"Hello, this is Samuel Constanza, from the Santa Maria de Chiquinquirá school," he explained for the farmer's benefit.

"Sam is that you?" the boss asked.

"Yes, I'm so sorry that we weren't able to contact you sooner, but we needed to get the children to safety first," Sam said, telling him that they'd gotten the children out of the compound before the raid. "There have been some complications, so if you could just send some help and maybe an ambulance here too…"

Sam handed the phone over to the farmer, who quickly filled Diego in on the address of his farm. Then he handed the phone back to Sam.

"Did you get that?" Sam asked.

"I did," the boss replied. "But be warned, it might take me a few days to get people over to where you are. We have been fighting fires on the home front ever since the raid."

"I understand, but please hurry. And please make sure that the parents know that their children are still alive, although one of them is seriously sick," Sam said.

"Noted, I'll be in touch with you soon," the boss replied, and the line went dead.

"Thank you so much," Sam said, handing the satellite phone back to the farmer.

The man replied with a suspicious grunt, still leading them back up into the forest towards his home.

Chapter Fourteen

IT WAS A SHORT WALK back to the man's farm, reaching a selection of buildings. They looked to have been built a while ago, but they were well-maintained. Even the barn had a fresh coat of red paint on it. Sam had been around the country long enough to know that wasn't always the case, especially in this area.

"You can settle into the barn over there," the man said, indicating to the building in question. "I'll ask my wife to get you something to eat."

"Thank you so much," Sam said, forcing a smile as the man disappeared into the main house.

"He's going to call the police," Ramiro said once the man was out of earshot.

"Probably," Sam agreed. "But there isn't much we can do. If we run into the woods, we won't be able to move fast and they'll find us for sure. Better just stay put and hope for the best."

"Do you have any money to pay off the cops if they come?"

Sam nodded. "Some, but probably not enough."

The farmer was true to his word, as almost fifteen minutes later, the man and his wife came out of the house toting a small table and some chairs. They went back into the house and fetched a *bandeja paisa*, a platter stacked with white rice, red beans, shredded meat, blood sausages, fried eggs, avocados and fried plantains.

Just the smell alone was enough to make Sam's mouth water, and from the wide-eyed looks from the kids, he could tell that they were in the same boat.

"Please, eat and drink, make yourselves at home," the stout and smiling woman said, helping the children to serve themselves. Water and what looked like cashew juice was being served as well.

Sam wasn't sure how they had managed to make that much food that quickly, but it was quite a feast. Sure, it wasn't high-class food, just the kind that workers ate to keep their energy levels up. It was tasty and filling, which was enough for them.

As hungry as Sam was, he couldn't take his eyes off of the farmer, who was watching them closely in turn. It wasn't difficult to tell what was going through the man's mind. He still doubted the story that Sam had given him, and the scared, hungry look of the children was the only reason why he had agreed to help. A good man, Sam thought. It would be a shame if they needed to kill him.

Finally, the car that the farmer was waiting for arrived at the gate, which the farmer jogged over to open. The car appeared to have no sirens or flashing lights.

Either the cop that was called in had come alone and not expected any trouble, or those that were armed and expecting trouble were waiting out of sight, just in case.

Ramiro narrowed his eyes, tensing up and looking like he was going to do something, but Sam shook his head. There was nothing that they could do right now that wouldn't get them in more trouble.

The man calmed down as the cop car drove in slowly, moving towards where the children were still sitting and eating.

The officer stepped out of the car, exchanged a few words with the farmer that the others couldn't make out. The farmer was talking quickly while pointing at Sam and the children.

Sam recognized the officer immediately. He was the one who showed up at the compound a few days before the raid, looking for a handout. The kind of officer who knew better than to make trouble for Sam's employer, although he would likely want compensation for the effort.

The officer also appeared to recognize him immediately and quickly worked to assuage the farmer's fears, making the gestures that meant for him to calm down and that help would be coming soon to collect the kids.

The officer quickly climbed back into his car and left, leaving the farmer looking a little puzzled. For the moment at least, he appeared satisfied with whatever the officer had said.

Sam and Ramiro both heaved a subtle sigh of relief.

Chapter Fifteen

A VAN ARRIVED the next day to collect them. Sam didn't recognize the driver, but the man had the look of those preferred by their employer. Young and recently released from an overly crowded prison to be given a renewed chance at a life of crime.

It was their transport, meant to get them out of the vulnerable position that the raid had put them in, and Sam said nothing as he took up shotgun position beside the driver. He maintained his silence as they headed back into the city, away from the forests that had been their hideout.

The food, water and rest had done Jamie some good, of course, and Sam could see him sleeping in the back seat. Not just unconscious as he had been back in the forest, but getting some actual rest.

He didn't like that he felt a little twinge in his chest at the thought, but there it was.

Sam wasn't sure about returning to the city, where cop cars often whizzed by. He felt exposed, riding in a van with these American children in plain view and the American cops looking for them.

No one seemed to notice, though, and they stopped outside what looked like a smaller house on the edge of the town. It was a suburb, and the house was large enough to accommodate all the kids, yet isolated enough not to have to worry about a neighbor noticing them.

Sam climbed out first, pulling the door open and letting the kids out one by one. When all the kids were through, the man approached Sam.

"How are you?" he asked. "Do you want some coffee?"

Sam shook his head. "Thank you. How…look, I'm sorry about what happened. We had almost no warning about the raid…"

"Don't worry about it, you did as you were meant to," the man said with a chuckle. "Quick thinking to pull the kids out before the cops got there. We'll need to be a little more careful now is all. The officer needed to alert the local police about the presence of the children, but he delayed it long enough to get you out. It's likely that the farm is already overrun with cops and American FBI. We have been lucky."

"I don't feel it," Sam admitted, rubbing at his sore arms.

"You will once you've had some rest," the boss said. "I'll stay here to help out, and make sure that the children are moved out again."

Sam nodded. "I appreciate that, sir."

"Of course," he said with a smile. "Now go. Get some rest. You've done good work. Once you've recovered, we have business to discuss. I've already got another buyer on the line, just waiting for us to fix our problems."

"Understood."

Chapter Sixteen

JAMIE WASN'T SURE how long they had been at the new place. After leaving the hideout, everything just felt a little fuzzy. It was difficult to tell how much time had passed, though one of the other kids told him that they'd been in the forest for about a week. It didn't feel like that long.

He was recovering, but he still needed lots of rest. They were in a safe location, and thanks to Sam's insistence, Jamie was allowed to rest for a very longtime over the first week or so. They were given good food, similar to the food at the farm, and he was feeling a great deal better.

Sam looked into Jamie's room and turned the light on, startling him and making him jump up from his bed.

"Come on," Sam said, motioning for him to move.

Jamie already knew better than to argue, quickly getting dressed and following Sam out to the car. Another kid was already in the car, waiting for them.

"A buyer?" Jamie asked, but there was no answer. The boss man was riding shotgun, and Sam drove them into the city. The buildings became taller, and more modern, and the cars were a little nicer, though the road was still bumpy.

They came to a halt in an alleyway leading to a dead end and a few doors leading into the nearby buildings. Another car was already there and a man was standing outside, smoking. He was about as tall as Sam but with lighter skin. He wore a dirty t-shirt and tattered jeans. As Sam parked and they all got out, the man crushed his smoke under a battered work boot.

Jamie already knew that he didn't like the man. Something about him creeped Jamie out; probably the way he stared at Jamie and the other kid as if they were pieces of meat, eyes wide and mouth agape.

He pointed at Jamie, who could feel his heart dropping in his chest as the boss man stepped forward and began to talk. Jamie was getting better at understanding Spanish, and he could hear that they were talking about money. The buyer was asking for a lower price, and the boss wasn't budging.

"No," the boss was saying. "And you trying to haggle is insulting to me. Sam, put them back in the car."

"Come on, it doesn't have to be like this..." the man said. He gave Diego a shove, nearly knocking him to the ground. Jamie jumped and tried running back to Sam, but he wasn't fast enough. Before anyone could react, the client reached out, grabbed Jamie by the arm and dragged him closer.

"Don't even think about it, *cabron*," the man said, seeing Sam quickly turning to help. Jamie could see a revolver in the man's hand, pointed straight at Sam. "I'm taking the boy. And you're going to let me. If not, someone's going to die here. Maybe you, maybe the boy." With the last remark he turned the gun toward Jamie and Sam nearly lunged at him but he restrained himself.

The boss got to his feet, saying something Jamie couldn't understand. It wasn't difficult to tell that he was angry, but Jamie had no idea what he was planning to do. It was difficult to focus on anything other than the man's grip on his neck, making it hard to breathe.

It all happened in a second. The client looked away, trying to get the car door open. Sam was suddenly moving, sensing an opening, and Jamie felt the weight of both men bowl him to the ground.

The sound of the gunshot was deafening, and Jamie covered his ears, screaming as three more shots rang out. The darkness of the alleyway made the gunshots flash brightly before his eyes.

When Jamie dared to open his eyes again, there was blood all over the place. The other kid was on the ground, clutching at his throat and choking. Sam was on the ground too, gripping at his stomach and groaning in pain. The buyer was down, too, but he wasn't moving. Jamie could see a pair of bullet holes in his chest. Diego was still holding his gun.

The blood had splattered on Jamie's cheek, and he wiped at it quickly with his sleeve.

"Get in the car!" the boss shouted. "*Puta madre,* get in the car now!"

Jamie wasn't sure who the man was talking to, but he turned to help Sam to his feet. Sam groaned softly, limping over to the van and pulling the door shut.

Chapter Seventeen

"HOW'S HE DOING back there?" The boss shouted.

Jamie realized that Diego was talking to him. They had driven away, leaving the buyer and the other kid for dead as police sirens grew nearer.

"Hey!" the man shouted. "Kid, how's he doing back there?"

Jamie jumped at the yelling. It was hard not to regress into the recollection of being pushed to the ground, the shooting and the flashing lights.

"He's… he's alive," Jamie answered in English. "He's breathing. There's blood."

"Where's the blood coming from?"

"His stomach!"

"Is he still bleeding?" the man asked, not looking away from the road. "Hey, kid, focus right now, is it still bleeding?"

Jamie wasn't sure how to tell. There was so much blood. Sam looked as if he was drunk, leaning against the seat and blinking slowly. Jamie pulled Sam's shirt up, and he groaned, his eyes rolled back and his head dropped to the seat. He saw that blood was still oozing from the gaping wound on the left side of his stomach.

"He's still bleeding!" Jamie said to Diego. "And... I think he passed out."

"Good, it means that he'll bleed less," the man said. "Find something to press into the wound to stop the bleeding. Do it gently but firmly, do you understand?"

Jamie nodded.

"Talk, boy!"

"Yes, I understand!"

He looked around, trying to find something to stop the bleeding. There was so much blood. All over the place. Jamie gagged, but pulled his own shirt off. It was a nice shirt, but already stained anyway.

He pressed his shirt onto the wound, gently, but firmly. He could feel the wet, heavy weight of the blood soaking into his shirt, but it didn't come through the fabric.

Something wet was on his hands. It wasn't the blood. Jamie almost didn't realize that he was crying until the tears started wetting his hands as he tended to Sam.

"How is he?" the boss shouted. "Is he still bleeding?"

"I... I don't think so," Jamie said. "He's still passed out, though."

"Just keep pressure on the wound, okay?" Diego said. Without waiting for a reply, he pulled his cell phone out and dialed.

Chapter Eighteen

ANOTHER CAR was already parked outside the house when they pulled in. Two men were standing outside. The van hadn't even come to a full halt when they yanked the door open and reached in to pull Sam out.

Jamie dropped back into his seat, staring as they carried Sam into the house, talking quickly in Spanish which he couldn't understand. The blood-soaked shirt dropped from his fingers to the floor of the car.

"Come on, boy," the boss said, climbing out of his seat. "Get in the house and get cleaned up."

Jamie didn't reply, simply jumping out of the car and rushing through the door after Sam.

Why weren't they just taking him to a hospital? Sure, people were looking for Jamie, so maybe he couldn't be sent to one, but why couldn't Sam be taken to a hospital? Who would be looking for him?

It didn't really matter. Jamie followed the men into the room, steeling himself as they started pulling out needles and IV bags, which they hung over Sam. They then started cleaning his wound.

They worked quickly but effectively. The bleeding had stopped, and they pulled out a bullet before stitching the wound shut.

The sight was almost enough to make him spew, but Jamie remained in place, watching in silence. He didn't even speak when the boss came along, with a garbage bag and told him to put his clothes in. He just stripped and put everything in the bag, then stood there watching over Sam until Diego made him go take a shower to wash the blood off.

When Jamie returned, they had finished the surgery, bandaged Sam's stomach and moved him to a comfortable cot to rest. Jamie sat beside him. Time passed slowly. Diego brought him ice chips to feed to Sam, who moaned, but he didn't wake up throughout the night.

***

WHEN THE BOSS entered the room, Jamie jumped up from his seat, pulling away from Sam and avoiding the man's eyes.

Diego's eyes were on Sam as he moved over to the bed and lightly ran a hand over the younger man's forehead. He seemed to genuinely care about Sam, somehow, or maybe it was all just a show. Jamie wasn't sure.

Without uttering a single word, Diego moved swiftly from the room and closed the door. Jamie returned to his place beside Sam, staring at the door for a few seconds before leaning back in his chair. Sam would be waking up soon, and Jamie would be at his side when he did.

He wasn't even sure why. The other kids had spoken about Sam carrying Jamie through the forest when he was unconscious, but Jamie didn't remember anything other than brief interludes. Maybe he just wanted to repay the favor.

Jamie sighed and tried to take a nap while Sam was quiet, having been up most of the night and suspecting he wouldn't be sleeping much again tonight. He was used to it at this point.

Chapter Nineteen

THE NIGHT WAS TOO QUIET. He had become accustomed to the cacophony of the forest at nighttime. Sure, the noises of the city outside could be heard here, but they were muted from inside the little room.

"Agua!"

Jamie jumped up from couch where he was sleeping, and looked around for the danger. But it was only Sam, gasping and sitting up in his cot. He was awake, conscious for the first time since passing out in the van three days before.

"What?" Jamie asked, looking around.

"Agua," Sam rasped, licking his chapped lips and coughing dryly. "Water, please."

"Oh, right," Jamie said, rushing from the room, and down to the kitchen to take a water bottle from the fridge. When he returned, Sam was laying down again. Jamie put the bottle on the bedside table.

It took him a few moments to realize the error in his ways and he picked the bottle up. He twisted the cap off and gently tilted Sam's head up, slowly pouring the water into his mouth. He was trying to be careful, but Sam coughed nonetheless.

"How are you feeling?" Jamie asked, but Sam didn't answer, settling back onto the bed, mumbling and groaning.

Jamie leaned forward, lightly pressing a hand to Sam's forehead, feeling the burning heat on his skin. He had a fever, and a bad one at that.

The doctor came along a few hours later to replace the bandages. Diego entered the room behind him and watched the doctor work.

Jamie tried to ask the doctor if Sam would be okay in Spanish, and he was relieved when the doctor chuckled.

"I speak English, boy," he said in a heavy accent.

"Right," Jamie grunted. "He had a fever last night. He woke up a couple of hours ago asking for water, so I gave him some. Was that okay?"

"Water is good," the doctor addressed both Jamie and the boss, who remained close to the door. "But if he doesn't wake up to drink it's okay. He's getting water from the IV. I'll give him antibiotics too, but if the infection has spread in his stomach... Well, I'd give him a fifty-percent chance of surviving the week."

Jamie blinked, not wanting to think about those odds. He watched as the doctor quickly packed his equipment. The boss handed the man some money on his way out.

Chapter Twenty

IT WAS ODD how the days passed so slowly. Jamie went back to sleeping in the bedroom with the other kids, but he spent every waking moment at Sam's side. He still wasn't sure why, or what he could do there. But he wanted to be there when Sam woke up.

Three days passed before he woke to see Sam sitting up in bed, drinking water and smiling at him.

"Good morning," Sam said, his voice still raspy. "Did you sleep well?"

Jamie blinked, unsure whether he was dreaming or not. He had dreamed a few times that Sam had woken, only to be disappointed upon waking.

But this was real. Jamie rushed to Sam's side, offering to help him with the water but Sam waved him away. He pressed a hand to Sam's forehead.

Sam chuckled, and coughed. "Diego said that you have been here almost the entire time, only leaving to sleep and eat when you had to. I appreciate that, although I'm not sure why you would… do something like that for me."

Jamie paused, taking a deep breath and shrugging. "I was scared you were going to die," he said, surprised that tears threatening to spill.

"Thanks for taking care of me," Sam said, and gave the boy a weak pat on the shoulder. "You know the boss wants to take you and the other kids out to meet more buyers now that I'm on the mend. The heat has mostly died down, so it should be safe to get you to…"

"No," Jamie said. "Not that again. What would have happened if that guy had had enough money to buy me? What would he have done to me?"

Sam nodded. "I've tried to talk him out of it. Wanting to keep you safe myself. Not sure how that would work out, but… I…"

"I understand," Jamie said. "You've been looking out for us as much as you could."

The older man smiled. "I was in a situation not unlike yours. I guess I needed some reminding."

"We could just run away," Jamie pointed out. "You're getting better now. We just take the van-"

"Shh," Sam said. "I'll think about it, but keep it quiet okay?"

Jamie paused, looking into the man's eyes, trying to figure whether he was speaking the truth or not. He couldn't tell. He never could tell when adults were lying to him, but in his gut, he felt that Sam was being genuine.

Sam smiled and nodded, looking like an idea was starting to come to mind. "Maybe it's a good idea, now that you mention it. But we have to go somewhere Diego won't find us. That'll be tough." He whispered.

Neither heard the light footfalls as the boss pulled away from the door. The man had heard enough, and he went outside, pulled his phone from his pocket and quickly dialed a number.

"This is taking too long," he said as soon as the call was answered. "I need to move these kids as quickly as possible, and with as little hassle as possible. Let me know your price… Yes, for all five. Tell me when you can pick them up."

Chapter Twenty-One

IT WAS SLOW GOING. A stomach wound didn't heal as quickly in reality as in the movies.

Not that Jamie ever really watched that many films involving that sort of thing. His parents wouldn't have approved, but he had managed to see a few grownup movies at his friends' houses. It all seemed so long ago now though.

Sam was getting better. Escaping from the man who wanted to take Jamie had cost him, though, and he was looking thin and pale as he got out of bed on shaky legs, and moved over to the window.

"How are you feeling?" Jamie asked, standing next to him and looking out.

Sam ran his fingers through his hair. He usually kept it clean shaved, but it had grown in thick and curly over the past few weeks.

"A little better, I think," Sam said and tapped lightly at his bandage. "Can't say I feel much better about it. Have you given any more thought to what we talked about?" he said quietly.

"You mean about getting out of here with the rest of the kids?" Jamie replied, also whispering. "Of course."

"I won't be able to move us out for a few more days, but with me being able to move on my own, I should be able to start planning," Sam said. "Diego hasn't been looking for more buyers, so that's a relief, but it's not going to last. We need to start getting a plan in motion."

Jamie nodded. "Any ideas where we could go? I don't know the area well, just what I've seen when we went to meet buyers."

"Don't forget the time we spent wandering the jungle after the police raided the compound," Sam said, shaking his head.

"I don't remember much about that," Jamie said.

"Well I remember carrying you most of the way," Sam said with a smile and ruffled his hair. "How are you feeling now? I know there were moments during that march when I was afraid for your life."

Jamie shrugged his shoulders. "I'm fine now. I'm glad you were there to carry me. I hope we can get out of here and live together. If my parents are dead…" he trailed off, looking down.

Sam narrowed his eyes, looking down at the boy. "Jamie, I don't know how it happened, but I have come to care a lot about you. But I've been your captor. That means… well, when we get right down to it, we can't really be friends, or even see each other once you're out of this. I'll make sure that you end up with someone that really will take care of you, but aside from that, we won't see each other. Hopefully ever again."

It physically hurt him to say that, for some reason, but as Jamie looked up at him, the kid appeared to understand, even if he didn't like it. Maybe a few months before, prior to his kidnapping and travelling down to Colombia, he would have been a little more emotional, but his experiences had forced Jamie to grow up prematurely. Sam remembered the same thing happening to him when he was about Jamie's age. He knew what it felt like.

The door opened, drawing their attention from the window and over to the boss at the front door.

"Jamie, get ready. You, Sherry and Lucas are being taken out to see a buyer," the man said, holding the door open for Jamie to rush through.

It left Sam alone with the man.

"Hope you're bringing some muscle this time," Sam said. "I don't think I'll survive another shooting."

"Just worry about the client, I'll have our backs covered," the man said, checking his gun. "They said that they only wanted two, but we've been taking care of these kids over a year and we need to move on from them, so try and force an up-sell. Get them to take all three, understood?"

Sam nodded. "Will do, boss."

The other man sighed. "I've been trusting you this far, Sam. I'm trusting you here, do you understand me?"

Sam narrowed his eyes at the man, but he nodded again. "Understood."

Chapter Twenty-Two

IT FELT LIKE FOREVER since Harry and Sharon had moved down to this hot, humid country in search of their missing son.

It had been over a year, and they knew the statistics but they refused to give up hope. They were going to find Jamie. A few of the missing kids had been found and brought home, safe and sound, but the last one was a few months ago now. The FBI said they were still on the case, but there were hearing from them less and less often and it seemed had mostly given up now. Harry had vowed that he would keep searching until he found Jamie, no matter how long it took, and he intended to keep that promise.

"Are you sure this is the place?" Sharon asked as he got back in the car beside her with a bag of takeout food.

"There's no being sure at this point," Harry said. "We've been on… how many of these stakeouts have we done again?"

"At least ten," Sharon said as Harry handed her a box of rice and fried beans. "But we have to keep on looking. There's really nothing else that we can do. Jamie is still out there waiting for us, and we have to keep on looking."

Harry sighed. He knew that she was right, and that Jamie was still out there, hoping for them just like they were hoping for him.

Sharon's faith had never wavered, no matter what. "A mother knows," she had told him probably a hundred times. If Sharon felt that Jamie was still alive, Harry would take that over any statistics that said his chances were less than one percent.

"But in this case, it is the spot that they told us about," Harry said. "Google maps says that we're here at this Calle Neustria Señora del Carmen, and that's where the informant said that it was going to be."

They were parked where they could keep an eye on the ins and outs of the place without being in direct view of anyone in the house. They'd been here most of the day and they hadn't seen anyone coming or going yet.

By the look of it, this part of town dated back to colonial days, with the bright paint jobs still intact in the area. The buildings were in good shape, and the area seemed middle class, which meant other cars parked around them. At least they stuck out no more than usual in this case.

"We're going to be fine," Sharon said, digging into her food. "We're going to find Jamie and head on home soon. I just know it."

Harry forced a smile, not feeling in the mood for food, but he knew the importance of eating, just to keep his own body going.

"I know, honey," Harry said, still smiling. "I know we will."

He was going to start believing that soon too.

Chapter Twenty-Three

IT WAS QUICK WORK to get Jamie ready, and the other two were already waiting for him in the car when he got outside. Sherry offered him a small smile as he climbed in. Lucas offered no gesture, simply staring ahead into space, like he wasn't going to be paying attention either way.

"Where are we going?" Sherry asked as Sam and the boss joined them, Diego taking the driver's seat this time.

"A couple that can't have children want to start a family," Diego said, not looking back at them as Sam pulled out of the driveway and onto the street.

Jamie felt like they were driving in circles, but they were soon stopped at a park, where Jamie could see a tall, lean, dark-haired man already waiting for them. He was wearing a suit and tie and was talking into a cellphone.

While they climbed out of the car, the man was obviously photographing Jamie, Sherry and Lucas with his phone.

"Don't worry, just sending some photos to my wife, who could not be here," the man said, although Jamie noted that he tucked his phone into an inside coat pocket without sending the pictures off.

"Sam, please keep an eye on the kids while I discuss the terms of our arrangement with Mr. Valdez," the boss said with a plastic smile, indicating for Sam to move away as he started speaking in Spanish. The man dressed like a rich guy and he was a little fat, not creepy like the last guy. Still, Sam looked a little wary, glancing over at him while watching the kids playing.

There wasn't much playing to be done, as none of the kids were in the mood. Instead they tried to listen to the conversation between client and boss. Neither Lucas nor Sherry appeared to understand the language, and they were speaking too quickly for Jamie to catch much.

It was still easy to make out that the man was pointing at Jamie and Sherry with a small smile. The boss shouted to Sam in Spanish before checking his own phone, smiling and shaking the client's hand.

They were directed back to the man's car, but Sam took hold of Lucas' shoulder, not letting him go. Jamie looked from the buyer to Sam.

Jamie tried not to cry, but he could feel the hot tears escaping from his eyes, running slowly down his cheeks as he stepped into the car with Sherry. They drove away.

He looked over to Sherry and without thinking, reached out and squeezed her hand, seeing tears in her eyes as well, though she too was trying to hide it.

Jamie knew he would probably never see Sam again. Now it was just him and Sherry.

Chapter Twenty-Four

IT WAS ANNOYING how long it took to recover from a gunshot to the stomach. Sure, Sam would have recovered quicker if they had taken him to a hospital for proper treatment.

But it would have also resulted in some uncomfortable questions from the hospital staff. People that worked in hospitals were required to report things like that, and likely wouldn't go for taking bribes to keep quiet.

But now the wound had mostly healed, so Sam planned to see a doctor about the pains he was still having in his stomach. He would have to make up a story about the wound, but he was getting good at lying by now.

Diego was in a good mood after successfully unloading two of the kids, but Sam felt terrible letting Jamie go without even saying goodbye. He made a note to track down the buyer and check on the kids later.

Diego dropped Sam at a nearby hospital before returning the remaining kid to their hideout. Lucas was quiet and glum in the backseat as they made the drive back to the house. Diego would normally have taken offense to the scowl on the kid's face, since surly kids were difficult to move, but he was in too good a mood to care about that for the moment. The silence was actually welcomed.

Most of the lights were out when he pulled into the driveway, coming to a halt in front of the house and stepping out of the car.

"Come on, kid, you need to get some food in you, and then bed," Diego said, shaking his head. "I'm not going to spend too long looking after you."

"Don't move!" shouted a man in English. This was followed by the unmistakable sound of a gun being loaded.

Diego looked around, his hand still on the door handle as Lucas was already out of the car and too far away for him to grab for a shield. Diego put up his hands and slowly turned around as an American man stepped out of the shadows, a revolver in his hands.

"Just my luck," Diego growled in Spanish.

A woman rushed out, corralling Lucas before he could get too far. "Oh, honey, it's okay, it's okay, and you're safe now."

Diego narrowed his eyes. He had been worried about the American cops coming for months, but these didn't look like cops. The woman had a soft look about her. The man with the gun was big and burly, with a beard and the calluses of a man who worked with his hands. Nope, these weren't cops, but they did have a gun. Amateurs were not to be underestimated. They tended to be unpredictable. But Diego watched carefully for an opening so he could draw his own gun.

"Where's Jamie?" the man asked, approaching Diego, as the woman joined them, quickly and deftly checking him and pulling the hidden pistol from his waistband.

"Where's Jamie?" the woman repeated, pointing his own weapon at him.

"*No hablo ingles*," Diego lied, shaking his head. It wasn't going to stand, but it would buy him some time.

"Bullshit," the man said, approaching slowly. They were amateurs, but Diego noted that this was far from the first time that they had done this. The parents of a kid that had been taken almost a full year before would have been at it for a while.

Diego just shrugged.

"Sharon," the man said. "Just call the police. They'll be able to do more than we can. Plus, they'll be able to figure out who this kid is."

Not the worst outcome, Diego thought as they indicated for him to sit on the ground. He was wearing an expensive suit, but he wasn't going to protest getting it dirty. No telling what amateurs would end up doing.

Chapter Twenty-Five

AS IT TURNED OUT, Sam and Diego hadn't been lying about how rich their new parents were. The man, who still hadn't introduced himself to the two children in his back seat, drove out of the city, heading up into the hills around it, moving out into a suburb filled with big, expensive looking houses with huge yards.

The gates opened automatically as the car moved into the driveway, and after almost a full minute of driving, they pulled up in front of a house.

And what a house. It was massive, at least three stories that Jamie could see. There was a lot of glass and white marble that made it look cool even in the blistering midday heat. They got out of the car and looked around uncomfortably as a young man in a white uniform offered to take the car but the man waved him away.

A woman came out of the house, looking confused.

"*Carlos, que pasa?*" she asked, eyeing the children.

"Maria, I wanted to surprise you," the man said, speaking almost flawless English. "Meet Jamie and Sherry. They were waiting for someone to adopt them at one of the local orphanages, and they really struck a chord in my heart."

Maria, a slim woman with black hair tied back in a ponytail behind her head, shook her head, but put on a brilliant smile as she approached the two kids. "Well, come on in, children, get out of the heat, I'll get you all something cold to drink, yes?"

Jamie and Sherry both smiled. The drive in had been air conditioned, but even a few minutes out in the midday heat made the idea of a cold drink appealing.

"You should have spoken to me about this first," Maria said as she poured the children each a glass of lemonade.

"Like I said, it was a surprise for you," Carlos repeated. "We'll talk about this when I get back from work, okay? I'm already late. I'll see you later, and then we talk."

He was out of the house and back in the car quickly. Jamie had the feeling that the man didn't want to have this conversation, leaving his wife staring with wide eyes at the two children who had suddenly landed in her lap.

Jamie looked around and finished his drink. He tried to force a smile. "Thanks for the drink, Mrs. Maria."

The woman laughed, the tension escaping her in that moment. "You're welcome… Jamie, right? Do you speak Spanish? Because my English is… how you say, not so good."

"I can understand some Spanish," Jamie said, looking around to Sherry who shook her head. "I can help to translate if you need it."

"I need to practice English too," Maria said with another laugh. "I was not expecting you two to be here, but I can ask the cook to make something for lunch, if you like?"

Jamie and Sherry both nodded enthusiastically. The food at the house in town hadn't been very good and they were both hungry for something better.

A cook. And there was a boy to valet the car. These people were richer than he'd thought, although he wondered why they were shopping around for children with the likes of those that had kidnapped Jamie and Sherry. And it was strange that Carlos had kept the situation a secret from his wife. And lied to her about where they had come from.

Jamie considered telling her about it as she turned around, calling the cook's name, but he doubted that it was going to do them any good. She wouldn't believe the word of a child she'd just met, especially not over that of her own husband.

Sherry drank her lemonade and smiled as Jamie squeezed her hand again.

"We're going to be okay," Jamie said, and she nodded.

She seemed reassured. He wished he could believe his own words.

Chapter Twenty-Six

THE POLICE HAD GOTTEN USED to seeing Harry and Sharon at their station, in search of updates or news on the investigation that they had moved to the back burner now that most of the international pressure had dissipated.

This was, of course, the first time that they had come with anything like results. The police weren't happy about the fact that they had been shown up by civilians, and tourists at that, but finding one of the lost children was enough to ingratiate the officers involved, and the man – Diego Vega was his name, according to the officers that made the arrest – was apparently wanted for a laundry list of crimes.

He was going to be processed, of course, but after some talking with the local police that were the most appreciative of their situation, Harry was allowed to sit in on the interrogation.

"I know that you have enough to hold me on," Diego was saying when they went inside. "But I can give up the ringleader, the man in charge of the kidnappings. He was the one calling all the shots. His name is Samuel Barrios, and he was actually with us today, but we dropped him off before returning to the hideout. I can give you his address, if you want. If he's not there, you can find him back at the hideout. He's been spending more time there."

The officer seemed amenable, offering the man leniency for his help, and Harry couldn't help reacting with a small scowl. He had been hoping for more questions about Jamie's whereabouts, but maybe this Samuel would have information about the rest of the children's whereabouts.

***

LEAVING THE DOCTOR'S OFFICE, Sam was still unsure whether the doctor believed that the wound to his abdomen was due to an accident, but it didn't really matter. The man had checked his wound to make sure that it was healing and that there was no infection. A packet of painkillers in hand, and he was on his way again.

It had been heartbreaking to watch Jamie be taken, looking as if he was trying to be strong but giving way to tears nonetheless. The sight was going to be haunting him for a while, but maybe he would be able to help Lucas get away now, and then try to find Jamie in his new home. Maybe he was in a good home, and Sam could just leave Jamie there. If not, he could take Sherry and Jamie to live somewhere else, and Diego would be none the wiser. He had already been paid, after all.

As he pulled in across the street from the hideout, Sam narrowed his eyes at the unfamiliar cars in the driveway. He had been evading law enforcement long enough to know an unmarked police car even in the absence of officers.

Had they found out about the hideout? Were more cops on the way?

Whatever the case, Sam didn't want to stick around and find out. He put the car back in gear and drove off before the officers across the street saw him.

Chapter Twenty-Seven

JAMIE WASN'T SURE IF HE TRUSTED MARIA just yet. She was an interesting woman and she appeared to be quite loving and affectionate to him and Sherry, but she seemed at a loss as to how to raise a child, leaving their care mostly to the servants they had at their beck and call. Unfortunately, the staff didn't speak English for the most part, and it was difficult to ask them for anything.

He definitely didn't trust Carlos. He was supposed to be the father in this crazy new family of theirs, but they didn't see much of him. He was around for breakfast, when he appeared to be perfectly nice.

Unless they spoke without being spoken to first. Or if they didn't reply when he addressed them. Or, if they chewed with their mouths open or slurped their soup. Jamie and Sherry quickly learned that it didn't take much to set the man off, and he had a bad temper. It was usually directed at the serving staff, and those that he yelled at appeared to be used to it, lowering their heads and backing away slowly as he verbally abused them in Spanish.

Thankfully, Carlos didn't spend much time with them, leaving Jamie and Sherry mostly to their own devices as Maria tried to figure out what she was supposed to do with the two children she had been saddled with. They were given their own room with nice, comfortable beds. The room even had a TV, with cable, but most of the channels were in Spanish. Jamie watched soccer games between teams Jamie had never heard of.

They were already in bed one night when they heard Carlos come home late. Despite the ample padding between them in their second-story room, they could still hear the muffled shouting from the first floor between Carlos and Maria, although he was doing most of the yelling.

Jamie gripped the side of his bed as he heard the shouting getting closer. They were coming up the steps.

He heard a soft, muffled shriek and the sound of a hand striking flesh, and his grip tightened, not wanting to get involved. Not that there was anything he would be able to do as a kid, but it infuriated him having to lie-down and pretend it wasn't happening.

The sound of springs moving drew his attention as he saw Sherry climbing out of her bed to join him in his. The bed was large enough to accommodate both of them, and Jamie didn't say anything as the shouting stopped.

Sleeping wasn't an option, however, and after a long night of tossing and turning, a staff member alerted them that breakfast was being served.

Sherry and Jamie used the bathroom and then joined Carlos and Maria in the dining room. They could see immediately that, while Maria was wearing a lot of makeup, there wasn't much that she could do to cover her fat lip.

Sherry paused behind Jamie, staring at the woman for a few seconds as Carlos came in behind them.

"Stare too long and maybe you'll get one too," he said with a cold laugh that only made Maria look down at her plate, clearly uncomfortable.

"What?" Jamie asked, feeling the back of his neck grow hot.

"I think we should go to the beach today!" the man suddenly declared. "What do you think? We can pack a lunch and spend the day out in the sun. I think that would be nice."

Maria stood up, forcing a smile. "I'll ask Joanna to get something prepared."

"Thank you," Carlos said, leaning in and kissing her cheek. "*Teamo.*"

Chapter Twenty-Eight

THE HOUSE WAS MOSTLY ABANDONED, but like the schools that had been raided back when the FBI was involved, it looked like it had been lived in recently. One of the rooms had been adapted into what looked like a hospital room.

"Do you think one of the kids was injured or sick?" Harry asked, and Sharon shook her head, not wanting to answer. Diego was apparently not going to be saying any more, at least not until they managed to find this Samuel character.

The hours were ticking by, afternoon turning to evening, and there was still no sign of Samuel. Those officers who had been sent to look at his house were having similarly bad luck. They did not enjoy the situation, but they had started to get used to it over their time looking for Jamie.

"Not our first stakeout," Sharon said, reaching over to squeeze her husband's shoulder. He felt tense and could really do with a massage. Maybe once they had found Jamie and got back home, they could do something about it.

"No, but hopefully the last," Harry admitted. "Just sitting and waiting for something to happen, hoping that something happens and kind of dreading it too... I can't say that I enjoy it."

"Can't wait for us to find Jamie and for all of this to be over," Sharon said with a small smile. "We can go home and be a normal family again. Probably have a ton of therapy fees, but it will be worth it."

He chuckled. "I don't know how you do it, honey."

"Do what?"

Harry shook his head, "Stay so positive, even after all this time."

"I have to," she said. "I can't contemplate the alternative. Are you hungry?"

He nodded, "Starving. I've actually grown to like the local food."

"Me too," she said, squeezing his shoulder again before standing up. The officers ushered her out in a way that would keep her from being seen.

She ordered food to go from a restaurant nearby, enough for them and for the officers escorting them. They packaged her food quickly and she was on her way in less than half an hour, finding her way to the back entrance through which she had left earlier.

Sharon narrowed her eyes as she walked through the door, not seeing any police officers. Or Harry. A sickening feeling came over her as she put the food down and slowly inched her way towards the door.

"Harry?" she called from the door, hearing her voice echo through the house, and not hearing a response. The bad feeling got worse when she looked to see the unmarked police car was gone. Where would they have gone? And why didn't Harry wait here for her?

"Harry, where are you?" she shouted again, walking around the house, assessing the moved and broken furniture, showing that there had been a struggle.

"Oh God," she whispered. "Oh God, Harry, where are you?"

Chapter Twenty-Nine

THE BEACH WAS A LOT CLOSER than Jamie realized, only a fifteen-minute drive.

He had never seen such a beautiful beach before, with pristine white sands and the ocean lapping at the edge in gentle waves. Other families were also there, enjoying the beachside restaurants, and men were pulling carts across the sand, trying to sell their wares to the people enjoying their day at the beach.

"This is the life, isn't it, kids?" Carlos asked, helping to carry the picnic basket. "Just some time playing in the sand and the water, good food, drink and spending some time out in the sun."

Jamie forced a smile and nodded, and Sherry did the same. He could tell Carlos only wanted agreement, not conversation, at least not with the kids.

Maria looked relieved that they were trying to keep the man placated. Jamie had the feeling that if they started acting out, she would be the one to pay for it, and while he didn't know her that well, he didn't want her to get hurt again.

Even so, he was still tired from lack of sleep the night before, and not in the mood for swimming. He hadn't brought any swim trunks with anyway. He sat in the sand, messing with the toys in front of him, staring out into the water. It was oddly relaxing with the waves crashing lightly on the white sand.

"All I'm saying is that you have already been through one bottle," Maria said, her trembling voice dragging Jamie out of his sleepy stupor. Sherry looked scared and moved a little closer so she could grab his hand.

"No, just speak your mind," Carlos said, in English this time, making sure that the children understood what they were saying. "Just tell me. Have you been counting my drinks? At the beach?"

"I'm just saying that you might want to pace yourself, considering that you drove us here," Maria responded also in English. "Not that I have been counting your drinks."

"You are counting my drinks," Carlos snapped, standing up and clenching his fists, his face taking on that flushed look. "And you don't like the way I drive, is that it?"

"No, that's not…" Maria started to say, inching away from him. Jamie felt that heat on the back of his neck again, holding onto Sherry's hand and squeezing a bit tighter than maybe was necessary as they watched the scene play out before them.

Carlos looked for a moment ready to get violent with Maria again, but he quickly looked around, seeing the other families watching them, albeit subtly, like they didn't want to get involved but still wanted him to calm down.

He shook his head. "I don't need this. I'm going."

He grabbed his shirt and the car keys, and quickly marched to the car, climbed in and drove away, leaving the three stranded and staring after him.

Maria looked stunned, as if she wasn't sure what had just happened. He had just left them stranded at the beach, but she looked relieved.

Jamie stood up, walked over to the first empty bottle discarded by Carlos and carefully tucked it back into the basket, quickly cleaning the sand from it first.

"Thank you, Jamie," Maria said with a small yet genuine smile. "You are a good child. You are both good children."

"No problem," Jamie replied, keeping his eyes downcast as he sat back down next to Sherry.

He kept his eyes downcast, but the warmth on the back of his neck receded when Sherry took his hand again, squeezing it back.

Chapter Thirty

HER HEART WAS HAMMERING as she drove through the colorful streets of Cartagena, looking around and trying to make herself seem as small as possible. Not only was Jamie still missing, but her husband was now missing as well.

"What the hell am I doing here?" she asked herself. She had no idea what she was doing, her only idea being heading back to the house that they had searched and found to be empty.

She had already called the local police to update them on the happening, but they were still too slow in mobilizing. There was no way that she was just going to sit around while her husband needed her help.

The house was small. Not quite an actual apartment, but it had a small driveway leading up to it. It was the size of an apartment, though.

She climbed out of the car, looking around for way in, trying to think of how to get in without setting off the alarm. Then she noticed the front door hanging ajar.

"Damn it," Sharon whispered. She knew she should have brought a gun but holding onto an illegal weapon with the police in close proximity had seemed like a bad idea at the time.

Sharon inched towards the door, pushing it open and looking around inside. It was a small place, with only the one bedroom, and the living room merged with the kitchen. The lights were all on, and the place seemed to have been ransacked, but what drew her attention immediately was the sight of Harry.

His hands were zip tied behind his back, and a couple more zip ties were used to tie his legs, leaving him all but hogtied on the ground, with an improvised duct tape gag over his mouth.

"Oh my God, Harry!" Sharon shouted as she rushed over to him, grabbing a knife from the kitchen to cut him loose. "Are you okay?"

His grumbling was muffled behind the gag before she pulled it off.

"I'm fine, just a little bruised is all," Harry said when she finally pulled his gag off. "The cops were called away and a few minutes later, a guy showed up. I think it was Sam, and they grabbed me and pulled out. I think that call was fake, which means that whoever this Sam person is, he's got a connection inside the police force here. We knew that they had connections," Harry said, rubbing some feeling back into his hands. "That's why we stayed away from the cops as much as possible."

"Well... I've already told them what happened, and they should already be looking for Diego," Sharon said, looking around the house. "What happened here?"

"They drove me here, beat me up, tied me up and left," Harry replied, shaking his head. "I'm still a little surprised that they left me alive. They were talking really fast in Spanish, so I think they were talking about it, but... they just left me here, just left me alive."

"Thank God for that," Sharon said, wrapping her arms around his shoulders, kissing his cheek. "There were just so many possibilities rushing through my head... I just thought that I'd lost you too..."

"Hey, honey," he said softly, stroking her hair. "I'm in this for the long haul."

"I know you are," she said. "You'd better be."

Chapter Thirty-One

"YOU'RE REALLY GETTING GOOD AT THIS!"

Jamie looked up from his paper to the young woman speaking to him. She spoke almost perfect English, despite her looks.

A tutor. They had hired a tutor to teach him and Sherry Spanish. It was at least a step in the direction of figuring out what they wanted to do with the kids they suddenly had.

After Carlos had abandoned them at the beach, things had changed. He came back a few hours later to find Jamie and Sherry swimming in their underwear while Maria watched. He apologized to Maria and took them to a nearby beachfront hotel for a nice pizza dinner and Jamie hadn't heard them fight since.

Either they were a lot quieter about it, and he was no longer hitting Maria, or they just weren't fighting. Jamie wasn't sure why people who fought like that would be married in the first place. His mom and dad had fights, too, but they had never hit each other.

After that, Carlos spent a lot less time at home, and Maria started getting into the actual parenting role of being a new parent. Maybe they were having a hard time because usually when people had kids, they started out with babies, and so things worked out differently.

A Spanish tutor was at least a step in the right direction.

Sherry was still having difficulty with Spanish, and while Jamie had been getting pretty good at speaking Spanish, reading had always been harder for him.

He shook his head. He'd never been great at Spanish in school, but a few things were coming back. The 'N' with a little squiggly line on top of it was one that he was never going to get right, though.

"Come on, Mr. Jamie, you're doing better than you think," the woman said with a small smile. "You just need to focus a little more."

"That's what my teachers back home said," Jamie grumbled.

"Back home?" she asked, tilting her head.

"I… never mind, I need to use the bathroom," Jamie said, pushing up from his seat. The woman smiled as she turned her attention to helping Sherry.

Jamie didn't need to use the bathroom; he just wanted to avoid the awkward questions. He started walking around the house. It was large enough for him to nearly get lost in.

Reaching the third floor, Jamie tilted his head. Someone was shouting in one of the rooms. It didn't seem to be with any kind of urgency. Nobody was in any trouble. It actually sounded more like grunts and moans.

He moved closer, leaning into the door to try and figure out if they weren't just talking and he didn't understand what she was saying. It was definitely Maria, but there was someone else in there with her.

The door moved as he leaned against it and it swung open. There was no creak on the hinge, but all thoughts of going unseen were dashed when the handle banged into the wall behind.

Maria was on her hands and knees on the bed, naked, with a tall, muscular man on his knees behind her, and both were looking up at him.

"Puta madre!" Maria shouted, jumping off the bed, quickly wrapping herself in the sheets and coming over to where Jamie was standing. "Jamie, get out of here!"

When Jamie turned to go, she called him back.

"Wait, I'm sorry I shouted. It wasn't your fault. You have to promise that you won't tell Carlos about this," she said, closing the door behind them. "Please?"

"Okay, I won't tell him," Jamie said, blinking.

"Promise!"

"I promise," Jamie snapped, pulling away from her tightening grip on his shoulder. "I promise."

"Thank you," she whispered, wrapping her arms around his shoulders. "Thank you so much."

"Okay," Jamie grunted, pulling away. "I'll just... get back to my classes now."

Chapter Thirty-Two

JAMIE HAD A FEELING that Carlos would eventually find out what was happening in that bedroom, whether he spoke up or not. They weren't trying to be quiet about their business, despite other people in the house, people who worked for Carlos.

A few days later, they were having their lesson again, and Maria once again disappeared.

Jamie heard the sound of the car pulling up the driveway. Carlos jumped out before it had even come to a full halt, looking red in the face as he tossed the keys into the hand of the valet and rushed into the house.

Jamie, afraid of what would happen if Carlos caught Maria and her boyfriend in the act, tried to delay Carlos in hopes that the boyfriend could slip out without getting caught.

Carlos walked briskly in the house and Jamie stepped in his path.

"Hey, Papa, you're home early," Jamie said, bringing the man to a halt. "Want to see how well we're doing in our Spanish classes? *Me llamo Jamie, y me gusta la pizza!*"

"That's nice," Carlos said, clearly not hearing a word. He stepped around Jamie and headed up the stairs, taking them two at a time. Once he reached the second landing, he was shouting Maria's name and what could only be a barrage of abuse.

The sounds of shouts and shrieks carried down to the first floor and Maria's boyfriend quickly ran down the stairs, a towel hastily wrapped around his waist and a bundle of clothes in one hand. Jamie and Sherry watched him run out the front door, not even bothering to close the door behind himself. A moment later they heard a motorcycle start up and roar off.

Jamie returned to his seat, but it was impossible to focus on his lesson with all the shouting going on. The tutor was well aware of that, but she seemed to be getting used to there being distractions.

"Well, children, why don't we move outside for the rest of the lesson?" she asked, forcing a smile and standing up from her seat.

"That sounds nice," Sherry said with a nod, looking over to Jamie before standing up as well.

"Getting away from the yelling match should be good if focusing is the idea," Jamie said.

"What is a yelling match?" the woman asked as they took their books out to the tables in the backyard.

"It just… nothing, never mind," Jamie said, dropping down onto the nearest seat. At least they had some shade to keep them out of the blistering heat of the sun.

He could still hear the shouting from inside, even if it was a little muffled.

Chapter Thirty-Three

HARRY AND SHARON went back to the police station. They knew Sam and the other men who had attacked Harry were long gone by now and it was doubtful they would be caught, but they had to let the cops know what happened anyway. Maybe they'd get lucky and the men would be caught and they'd lead them to Jamie.

The police of course claimed they were doing everything they could, scouring the city for Diego and Sam.

"They're not going to find them," Harry said softly as he handed Sharon a cup of coffee. "If they have someone on the inside showing them where not to go, they'll just lay low in the city and wait it out."

"Have a little faith, okay?" Sharon said, rubbing her husband's shoulder. "This is the closest we've been to finding Jamie all year, and we're going to keep on getting closer. We just have to believe that it'll work, okay?"

Harry nodded, taking a sip of his own coffee. If there was one thing that he could say in favor of this place, it was that they brewed some of the best coffee he had ever tasted.

An officer came over to them, pulled up a chair and sat across from them as he scratched lightly at his five o'clock shadow.

"Well, we have been speaking to the boy Lucas about what happened to him while we wait for his parents to make contact," the man said. "He was taken from the west coast of the USA, Portland, I think the city name is, and he knew the number to call them from, so we should be hearing back from them soon. You saved his life, more likely than not."

Sharon smiled, patting Harry on the shoulder. "You hear that? That kid's going back to his folks because of us."

He nodded in response, placing his hand over hers. "Did he know anything about our Jamie?"

The officer nodded. "He remembered Jamie. A younger child with brown hair. He and one of the girls were handed off to someone else a few days ago, and Lucas knows this because the man was asked to pick between the three of them and chose the boy that we assume for now was your son, and the girl. He remembers the time and the place of the handoff, and he took down the license plate of the car that took them, hoping that he would be able to pass it on, he says. We are looking through security footage of what happened right now. There weren't many cameras around the park itself, which is why they picked that area, but there should be a few that are around the park that might be able to help us in identifying and tracking both the people that were involved on both sides of the deal. We will be keeping you in the loop of what we find, but for the moment, I think you two should go back to your hotel and get some rest."

Harry looked over to Sharon. She did look exhausted. It had been a long few days since they had gotten their hands-on Diego and brought him in. While they did feel like they were closer to their son than they had ever been before, they did need to get some rest.

And she agreed. "Thank you so much, officer, I think we'll go ahead and do just that."

Chapter Thirty-Four

THEY WERE FINISHED WITH THEIR CLASS for the day and Sherry was riding the bicycle that Maria had bought them to ride around the house, when they could hear things starting to get worse inside. There was yelling, things being broken and thrown around, and even a few of the windows smashing.

Being outside didn't feel right, too exposed somehow, so he and Sherry found their way into their room, where Sherry curled up on his bed once more. She wasn't going to be sleeping, not even as night was falling, and Jamie wasn't either, most likely. He was sitting up, with his back to the head of the bed and his eyes on the door as the shouting continued. Dinner time came and went, but they weren't hungry.

It wasn't long before they could see Maria leaving from their window, picking up one of the cars and driving off into the night. She was clearly distressed, the bruises and cuts evident on her arms and face even from their second-story window. Carlos yelled at her from outside for a few minutes before returning inside.

They could hear him yelling and throwing things for a few more hours until the house fell into an awful silence.

Jamie wasn't sure which he preferred. The shouting was difficult to live with, sure, but the silence was almost like a shroud hanging over them, not letting them breathe.

The hours ticked by, and Jamie caught himself nodding off a couple of times until the sun was starting to come up and he leaned over to nudge Sherry in the shoulder.

She had nodded off, but was instantly awake, looking around with wide eyes, but calming down quickly when she saw that she was alone with Jamie.

They were both hungry, and the house had been quiet enough for a while, leaving them feeling safe enough to head downstairs to see what was happening and maybe get a bite to eat.

The living room was in complete disarray. They could see Carlos lying on a couch, snoring loudly and surrounded by bottles of beer and spirit bottles.

Both were careful not to make a sound as they reached the kitchen. The staff were not yet in, likely not wanting to be around when Carlos woke up, giving them free reign to grab a couple of bowls, a carton of milk and a few of the sugary cereals before climbing back up the stairs to their room.

Jamie could understand why Sherry wouldn't want to say anything. So much as making a peep at this point felt dangerous to them both, especially if Carlos woke up.

But they were too hungry to care, and Jamie found himself quickly pouring himself another serving of the cereal. The jittery feeling in his fingers was starting to go away and they felt a little safer than anywhere else in the world here in their room.

Eating cereal in bed. His parents would die of shock if they ever found out. If they were still alive.

The sun was still climbing in the sky, but only had an hour or so to go before they heard any movement from below. Both hoped and prayed that it would be one of the serving staff starting to clean up, but as they could hear the heavy steps coming up the stairs towards them, those particular hopes were dashed.

"It's going to be okay," Jamie said, wrapping Sherry in his arms as the footsteps stopped outside their door to be replaced with a hammering at the door.

"I know," Sherry whispered back.

Chapter Thirty-Five

THE DOOR WASN'T LOCKED, of course, but it took Carlos a few tries to get it open. Maybe he wasn't sure who was inside the room. Maybe he thought that they would have locked the door. Jamie would have, but there was no key in the door.

He pushed the door open, with large, dark circles under his bright red eyes, his fingers still clawing for the door handle as it swung open a little too quickly.

Carlos looked grumpy and hung over the way that Jamie remembered both his parents being after New Year's, but he did not seem quite as upset as he had been the night before. Then again, Jamie knew for a fact that it didn't take much to set the man off.

Sherry appeared to know the same, and neither were going to say anything until Carlos spoke. It didn't sound quite right, but Jamie didn't want to have to deal with the man throwing things again.

"*Vamos al puta coche de mierda,*" Carlos said, slurring his words a bit as he looked around the room.

"What?" Sherry asked, looking scared and confused.

"I think he wants us to go to the car," Jamie said. "I'm not sure what some of the words were, but I know they were foul."

"Good to know that those classes were good for something, at least," Carlos growled, rubbing his temples and then his eyes as he looked away from the bright sunlight streaming in through the window. "The boy is right. You're getting into the car right now, and we're going out for a ride. You're going back to where you came from, since I don't have a wife to surprise anymore."

Jamie wasn't sure how that worked out, but they weren't going to be questioning it or him for the moment. He did look like he was one wrong word away from getting him into throwing a fit again, and Jamie didn't want to find out what he was capable of when he didn't have Maria around to contain him.

They went out to the car, where Carlos seemed to be still a little too drunk to be driving, but they were heading back the way that they'd originally come. Jamie couldn't help but feel a little excited over the prospect of seeing Sam again.

At least, that was what he assumed Carlos meant when he said that they were going back to where they'd come from.

They pulled up in front of a small house inside the city, where Carlos climbed out, cursing again as the door was clearly opening. That was never a good sign, Jamie thought, squeezing Sherry's hand in his as Carlos disappeared into the house.

"He's pissed off," Sherry said softly. "What do you think he's going to do?"

Jamie shrugged his shoulders. "I don't know. But I don't think I want to find out."

Sure enough, it appeared as if Carlos hadn't found what he was looking for inside the house, and he came out looking angrier than before, cursing loudly before climbing back into the car.

"What are you looking for in there?" Jamie asked Carlos once he was seated behind the wheel of the car again.

Carlos snapped, turning back around and back handing Jamie across the cheek.

Jamie pulled away, cowering over Sherry to make sure that Carlos didn't attack her as well even though his cheek was stinging from the strike.

"You don't talk to me," Carlos roared as he turned back around to start the car up again. "You knew that slut was cheating, and you didn't say anything."

Jamie could feel a few tears slipping down his cheek as the car engine roared to life, but he refused to cry openly.

That would only worsen the man's already bad mood, he just knew it.

Chapter Thirty-Six

AFTER A FEW MORE STOPS, Carlos eventually gave up the search for the day, taking them back to the house and dropping them off before driving off again. Jamie wasn't sure if the man was going to be searching for Sam some more, or if he was just going to get something to drink. He had torn through the supply of liquor inside the house, after all.

The household staff had already cleaned the trashed areas of the house. Or at least started to, since the man had made quite a mess.

The kitchen staff had managed to whip something up for them to eat, but none were willing to so much as make eye contact with either of the children. What happened the day before was still hanging over the house, and likely would for a long time to come.

But if Carlos had anything to say about it, they weren't going to be dealing with that for too much longer.

Once Jamie and Sherry were finished with the beans, rice and eggs that had been whipped up for them, they headed up to the bedroom.

Sherry was in Jamie's bed again, and they both managed to get some sleep, knowing that Carlos was out of the house. Jamie's dreams were plagued by nightmares, waking him up time and time again, but there was little that he could do but turn over and try to get some rest.

Carlos' car pulled up again early in the morning, bringing a new girlfriend, a woman that looked a good deal younger than Carlos. Over the next few nights, they drank and trashed the house until Jamie and Sherry both learned to stay inside their room whenever Carlos or the woman were in the house.

Thankfully, the two seemed more than willing to ignore the kids in their house and leave them and their room be.

They weren't comfortable being cooped up in the room anymore, and the tutor didn't come around to teach them Spanish anymore. Jamie tried to help keep Sherry's mind off of their predicament by using the books that they still had to teach her what little he knew.

It proved to be of some help, giving them something to do in the house while Carlos and his new girlfriend were in residence. It wasn't a pleasant arrangement, but all in all, it did seem to work.

A few days into the new rhythm that they were adjusting to, Jamie jumped out of his bed at the sound of the bedroom door opening in the middle of the night. There wouldn't have been much that he could do against someone as large as Carlos, but damned if he wasn't going to do his best.

Carlos stood in the door for a few minutes, surprised that Jamie was already up, and then he laughed.

"You two have five minutes to get everything packed up," he growled, scratching at a beard starting up on his cheek. "There are some bags in the closets. Pack and be ready to leave. You're going back. About damned time, if you ask me."

He closed the door, and Jamie turned to see Sherry hiding under her blanket.

"Come on, you heard him," Jamie said. "Let's grab anything that they gave us, and pack it, just in case we go somewhere that doesn't have quite as much."

Sherry nodded, quickly climbing out of bed and following his lead.

Five minutes later, they had crammed most of what they had been given into the bags. Carlos came back with two men, who grabbed the bags and the kids by their arms and dragged them outside.

It was still warm outside, warmer than it was inside the air-conditioned house, but it still didn't help the chill running down Jamie's spine as they were pushed into the van waiting for them, and it drove off.

He grabbed Sherry's hand and squeezed. She squeezed back without saying a word.

Chapter Thirty-Seven

"ARE YOU SURE ABOUT THIS?" Sharon asked as they drove up to the massive mansion outside the city.

"Yes, I'm sure," Harry replied, looking tense. "This is the address that the owner of the car that Lucas saw lives in, or that's what the officer told us. What was his name again?"

"Ramirez, I think," Sharon said, shaking her head. "And that's not what I mean. We know that this is the place, but the police know too. If they're going to be mounting some kind of operation to get Jamie back, shouldn't we just let them do their job?"

"It'll take them days to get a warrant like that, if there's a mole inside the police force, the owner of this place will be long gone by then, and so will Jamie. We need to act now."

Sharon took a deep breath. She knew that he was right, and there was really no turning back now. They weren't going to be letting Jamie slip away, not when they were so close. Not this time.

They pulled up to the front of the house, since the gate had been left open, and made their way over to the front door together. Harry knocked and rang the doorbell.

A few minutes passed before the door was opened by a younger, lean-looking man with bags under his eyes and an ugly beard starting on his chin. He said something in Spanish.

"What?" Sharon asked.

"I said you're not the pizza delivery guy," the man said in near-perfect English. "Who the hell are you?"

"My name is Harry, and this is my wife, Sharon," Harry said. "And you have my son, Jamie, here, and another girl, too. Hand them over to us, and there won't be any trouble."

"Trouble?" the man asked with a laugh. "No, no children living here. I don't even have a wife, just me and my girlfriend."

"Could we ask her if she's seen them?" Sherry asked.

"She doesn't speak English," the man replied, suddenly evasive.

Sharon's eyes flickered over to the yard in the back. She could see a basket full of beach toys out in the open, as well as a bright pink children's bicycle with red tassels hanging from the handlebar.

The man saw their eyes looking over to the evidence of his lies, but before either of them could do anything, Harry realized that there was a revolver in his hand. He quickly pushed Harry back a few steps before pointing the gun at them.

"*Puta Madre* Americans think that you can just walk in and do whatever you want," the man snarled. "I'm calling the police."

"Yeah, you do that," Harry snapped back, raising his hands. This wasn't the first time he'd had a gun pointed at him, not even the first time this week.

Harry and Sharon got in their car and drove out of the long driveway, then parked outside the gate.

"Lucas said there was a little girl with Jamie, right?" Sharon asked.

"Yeah, a girl named Sherry," Harry said. "I'm guessing that was her bike. When the police search the place, we'll find out if Jamie was here or not."

***

ONCE THE POLICE arrived, however, it didn't look like they were interested in the bicycle or in anything Harry and Sharon had to say. An unmarked police car drove past them without stopping and approached the house. Harry and Sharon followed in their own car but they didn't get out. They watch Carlos come out of the house and speak to the police, still holding his gun in his hand. The conversation was brief and Harry and Sharon didn't understand enough for it to make sense, but the body language of the police officers made it clear they weren't here to confront Mr. Ramirez. Instead, they looked almost apologetic, like they were here responding to his complaint, which, Harry supposed, was exactly what they were doing. Ramirez had been the one to call them, after all.

The officer approached them after Carlos went back in the house. They recognized the man from their visits to the police station. He was a detective and he spoke English well. He was taller than average for Columbians and he had a muscular build; he had a full head of hair and he looked to be about Harry and Sharon's age, but a closer look at his face revealed he was probably ten years older than them.

"I'm sorry it turned out this way," the officer said. "But this man, Carlos Ramirez, is very important and very rich in this area. His father is on the city council. He has made sure that there are orders to escort you from the city, and if you ever return, you will be arrested."

"Us arrested?" Harry roared, turning red in the face. "He's the one that had our son."

"It's how this happens here," the officer said, lowering his head and his voice. "I need to ask you two to follow me to the airport."

"We are going to find our son," Harry shouted. "I'm not letting anyone stop us. I'll die before I'll give up."

The cop didn't reply, but his hand moved toward the gun holstered on his belt. Harry decided it was best to get in the car and live for another day; they could go back to searching for Jamie tomorrow.

"This is just a minor setback," Sharon said as they drove out the gate again. "We're closer than we've ever been to finding Jamie. I can feel it. I think it's time we contact Agent Harper again and see if they can't come and check this guy out."

"I hope you're right," Harry said. "Only problem is, by the time the FBI gets here, Ramirez will have gotten rid of all evidence that Jamie was ever here. If he was here."

Part Three

Second Hand

Prologue

SHERRY GRIPPED JAMIE'S HAND throughout the drive. She had a firm grip, and he could feel her nails digging into his skin. It hurt a bit but he didn't have the heart to break her hold. They needed each other now, more than ever, and he was going to be there for her, in whatever way he could be.

The van traveled through the night, heading through the hills outside of the city, though they could still see the lights in the distance. They appeared to be making lots of turns, as if they were trying to avoid the main roads, instead using less-traveled side roads which had lots of potholes. These roads likely had fewer police patrolling, Jamie thought.

Talking with Sam while the man had been recovering had certainly been instructive on how the criminal element worked in a city like this. A city like Cartagena, Columbia. One that, as an 11-year old American boy, he shouldn't know much about.

They finally started heading back into the city, moving close to the tall buildings that marked the city center. They pulled into an alley behind a tall building on the edge of town, then stopped in front of a large door, which slowly rose to admit the van.

Jamie looked over to Sherry, who still looked a little scared, but they didn't appear to be in any immediate danger, even as they moved down into the underground garage of the building.

The van came to a halt and the men outside were speaking quickly in Spanish, too quickly for Jamie to understand. Jamie and Sherry were dragged from the van with their hands secured behind their backs with plastic cable ties. One of the men opened a steel door with peeling paint, revealing a staircase which they started walking up.

"Where are we?" Sherry asked, looking around as they marched up the interminable flights of stairs. No one answered her.

As they passed the doors leading into the different floors, Jamie caught sight of carpeted hallways, with doors on either side with numbers on them.

"I think we're in some kind of hotel," Jamie replied, and Sherry looked up to him, her bright brown eyes wide. "We're going to be okay. I'm going to be with you."

As they stepped out of the stairwell into a hallway, Jamie realized that Sherry was being held back from following him.

"No!" Jamie growled, pulling out of the man's grip.

The man laughed, reaching down to grab at Jamie's arm again as he tried to get back to the stairs.

"No, Sherry!" Jamie shouted, shrugging the man off, and when he tried to grab again, Jamie turned back, seeing the man with his head lowered.

Jamie jerked his head forward and felt the man's nose connect with his forehead. It made a loud, satisfying crack.

"Puta madre!" the man shouted, clutching at his bleeding nose. Jamie didn't know exactly what this meant, but it was a bad word and had something to do with mother. The other men reached out to grab him.

He tried to kick them away, tried to hit another with his head. When they tried to cover his mouth to stop his screaming, Jamie bit at their fingers.

All he could see were Sherry's wide eyes, watching as he tried to fight them off. They were all adults. They were bigger and stronger than he was, certainly bigger than Sherry, who was a year younger and a fair bit smaller than him. And there were four of them. But he had to try anyway. He wasn't going to let them separate him from Sherry if he could help it.

"Kill this little coño!" one of the men shouted, and Jamie pulled free, trying to reach the door.

More hands grabbed his shoulder, and as Jamie tried to wriggle free of their grip, he felt something prick him in the neck. It felt like a bee sting, almost imperceptible in the state that he was in, but a few seconds, he could feel himself losing control over his limbs.

His vision blurred, and the door closed between him and Sherry.

"No… Sherry…" he tried to say, but it felt like he was talking through a mouthful of cotton.

He was falling back. He could see the ceiling now instead of the closed door. He tried to say something, but nothing came out.

More hands reaching for him. Blackness.

Chapter One

JAMIE KNEW THIS FEELING all too well. The feeling of being drugged

He opened his eyes slowly and let out a soft groan while turning over in his bed. There were a horde of aches and pains all over his body, but the dryness in his mouth and the dull, pounding headache were signs that he had been drugged. He tried to remember where he was or how he had gotten there, but his mind was all mixed up.

He'd felt the same way when he woke up on the submarine after being kidnapped from his school in Massachusetts. Jamie rubbed his temples in an attempt to get rid of the pounding in his head, or at least give it a bit of a rest as he pushed up from his bed.

He had no real memory of having arrived in this place.

As the realization dawned on him, Jamie blinked a few times to adjust his eyes to the darkness around him. He was in a room with a group of bunks, most of which were empty, except for one where he could see a boy about his own age asleep.

With a soft groan, Jamie pushed himself up from the bed, feeling the world spin around him for a few seconds. He maintained a grip on the top bunk above him to keep from falling over, then a sweeping sense of nausea hit him.

"Great," he grumbled under his breath. "First thing I want to do is throw up…"

But nothing came, and the sensation passed in a few seconds. Eventually, the world stopped spinning, and he was able to stand up normally.

His mouth was still dry and tasted like sour milk. The room around him smelled even worse; he picked up some strong body odor and the distinct, sharp smell of cigarette smoke, mixed with a strong, sour smell that he couldn't identify. The combination made him want to throw up again.

He still felt like nothing was going to come up though, and after a few minutes of recovering on his feet, Jamie was finally able to walk around the room. He walked quietly, since he didn't want to wake the sleeping kid. As he moved around, he started to feel a little better, and the memories of the trip here started trickling back. Carlos kicking them out in the middle of the night, the long trip in the van. Sherry.

"Sherry," Jamie said aloud, suddenly feeling his heart race. He forgot all about being quiet. "Sherry!"

He needed to find her. The kidnappers tried to separate them, but Jamie had fought back, for all the good that it had done.

The room and shared bathroom appeared to take up the entire floor, since the only other door he could see led into a stairwell. Memories of living with Carlos came back as he quickly walked down the stairs. It hadn't been great dealing with Carlos's anger almost every day, especially after he'd kicked out Maria, so Jamie had been glad to get out of there. But was this place worse? What was this place?

He moved down the steps, rubbing his sinuses. That was going to annoy him for a while; he knew that from being drugged before.

There was nothing about this place that Jamie liked and the sour smell was following him everywhere he went. It now reminded him of milk that had gone bad.

"Maybe this place was a milk factory or something," he thought to himself, reaching the next floor. The stairs kept going down for at least another five floors, but Jamie wasn't sure what he would find at the bottom. When he reached the bottom there were voices coming from beyond the door. He leaned in closer, narrowing his eyes, trying to figure out what he would find in there.

He would need to talk to someone to find out where Sherry was. He needed to get away with her; maybe together they would find a way to get back home.

Jamie took a deep breath and twisted the handle.

Jasper Joshua West

Chapter Two

THE DOOR CREAKED loudly and shuddered against the rusty hinges, making Jamie's entrance as loud and conspicuous as possible. Even so, it didn't seem to attract much attention. There was already a great deal of noise coming from inside the room, and those closest to the door briefly glanced over to see him, but the rest appeared too enthralled in their own business to really care.

It looked like a common room, shared amongst a group of about fifty other children. Most of them were seated on long benches in front of wooden tables, talking and playing cards. There were six adults in the room too, but they were all siting together on the far side. Some of the adults were also playing cards but others just sat smoking, or drinking. A TV was on a table near where the adults were sitting, but no one seemed to be watching as it burbled away in Spanish, not loud enough to be heard over the din of kids talking. The adults seemed to put as little interest in their apparent job of watching over the children as was possible, only glancing briefly up to scan the room then returning to their own conversation.

The kids were mostly girls, and from what he could tell, some appeared to be around his age, some a few years older. The boys were older, about 13 or 14, he thought, looking at their faces which had pimples and bits of facial hair. They were also bigger than Jamie. It was the boys who looked up as Jamie walked through the room, but after a brief glance, they quickly turned back to their games.

Maybe they just thought that Jamie wasn't big enough to pose a threat. As far as he could tell, he was the only American; most of the children had the dark skin, hair and eyes of Latinos.

"Sherry?" Jamie called, barely able to get his raspy voice above the din around him. Jamie was starting to feel a little desperate now. He moved through the crowded tables, trying to find the girl he had promised to protect, no matter what. He wasn't sure if it was a promise that he could keep, but he was going to do his best.

"Have you seen a girl?" Jamie asked one of the smaller groups, but they ignored him. "Her name is Sherry, have you seen her? She's ten, with curly brown hair, freckles on her nose?" He thought for a moment, then added, "She's American," which made a few of the boys laugh. That meant at least some of them understood English but were just ignoring him.

Jamie tried again, this time speaking in his broken Spanish. Finally, one of the adults on the far side of the room saw him and walked over.

The man wasn't tall, but he looked strong. He had a thick black mustache and a hard-looking face. He wore a t-shirt with the sleeves torn off, revealing big muscles and plenty of tattoos. Jamie could see a large knife in a sheath attached to his belt, and when the man placed a hand on Jamie's shoulder, his first instinct was to pull away, but his grip was too firm.

"You come with me," the man growled. He wasn't asking. He pushed Jamie over to and through one of the doors near to where the other men were sitting.

There he found Sherry lying on an old leather couch. He pulled away from the man's grasp and rushed over to her. When he put a hand on her shoulder, she stirred and opened her eyes.

"Jamie?" she asked, blinking slowly, needing a second to see him. "I thought… you fought with the men… are you okay?"

"What did you do with her?" Jamie snapped, looking back at the man still standing at the door.

"She scream, we give her medicine to sleep," the man said, then chuckled "Here, kids have no mama, no papa. New home here, okay?"

Jamie didn't answer. He turned back to Sherry and held her hand in his, feeling the relief washing over him like an overwhelming wave. At least they were together.

"Are you alright?" Jamie asked, wiping sweat beads from her forehead. "Did they hurt you?"

She shook her head slowly. "No, I'm not hurt. I feel sleepy and a little sick, that's all."

"It's the drugs," Jamie said softly. "Just take it slow until they wear off. Are you thirsty?" He looked around for the man who had brought him in, but he was gone. Another man was tapping away at his phone, ignoring him and Sherry.

She nodded, smiling and leaning into his hand. "I'm glad you're okay and we're still together."

"Yeah," Jamie said softly. "So am I. But where are we? What is this place?"

Chapter Three

IT TOOK A FEW HOURS for the drugs to wear off. When the men brought in food, the smell made Jamie's stomach growl. He couldn't remember when he'd eaten last, but his stomach was completely empty now.

It was just rice and beans, but it was hot and filling; Jamie and Sherry found themselves attacking their plates and getting a second helping from the large pot which sat on a table in the middle of the room.

Jamie wasn't going to leave Sherry's side again, he vowed. He was going to do everything that he could to make sure that she was safe. They would have to kill him if they wanted to separate them again. They hadn't known each other long, but what they had been subjected to over the past few months had resulted in them forming a bond that was unbreakable.

Once they were finished eating, the children were quickly directed up the stairs towards the same room full of bunks where Jamie had woken a few hours ago. Most of the children appeared to readily jump to the orders, making Jamie wonder why they weren't fighting back. There weren't as many people here, and Jamie didn't know where the other people had gone, but there were at least thirty kids and only four adults. But everyone followed orders. Maybe they were beaten if they disobeyed, he thought.

Jamie's only responsibility, as he saw it, was to keep Sherry safe. As he had done at Carlos's house, he started thinking about how he could escape, but this time, he needed to take Sherry with him. He didn't know what all the girls were wanted here for, but he got the feeling it wasn't good. No way would he leave Sherry here alone, not even if he was going to get help.

They were separated quickly into groups of boys and girls and then guided into large bathrooms on opposite sides of the room. They boys' room had a line of six showers on a single wall. There was no privacy and no walls, but Jamie was used to that by now from his time at the hideout in the forest. The boys stripped down and put their clothes in piles on a wooden bench, then waited their turn in the showers. Jamie followed suit, joining the end of the line. The six shower heads all ran continuously and as each boy finished and left, he was immediately replaced by the next boy in line. When they finished, the boys each grabbed a tattered towel from a heap on a table, dried off, tossed it in the basket and went back to the bench where they had left their clothes. One man stood looking bored by the table with the towels, holding a piece of wood about the size of a baseball bat but that looked more like a table leg. There wasn't any trouble, but this man appeared to be ready.

Noting the body hair now visible on the other boys, Jamie confirmed his suspicion that he was indeed the youngest, and probably the weakest. Some of these boys might be older than he thought. Would he be able to protect Sherry?

Jamie finished up, left the bathroom and quickly found Sherry in the crowd, and stayed by her side. She seemed happy to see him, and grasped his hand in hers as they chose bunk beds in which to sleep.

Like the showers, the bunk beds were designated for boys and girls, but as Jamie was unwilling to part with Sherry again, they chose two free beds in the middle of the room which formed the dividing line between the two sections.

That didn't go unnoticed by the others. A few moved over to where Jamie and Sherry were setting up, watching them closely.

"What are you looking at?" he snapped, turning to face them.

A few of them, mostly girls, quickly backed away, but those who remained came a little closer.

"I'm Juanito," one of the boys said in English. He had his hair shaved almost down to his scalp, and he looked about thirteen years old. "We're just wondering…"

"She's my sister," Jamie lied.

"Oh," Juanito said, scratching his head. "Well, you don't want to be around her when they take her out for a ride. They maybe take you too, you know? Young gringo boy, maybe rich men think you're cute, no?" The other boys laughed at this and spoke amongst themselves in Spanish.

"Where will they take us to for a ride?" Jamie asked, feeling his stomach sinking a bit as the other boys around Juanito started making rude gestures. The one that seemed pervasive was a forefinger pushing into a circle made by the other hand's thumb and forefinger.

"I won't let them take her," Jamie growled, moving back to the bed.

"If you say so," Juanito said, shrugging. He looked like he didn't believe Jamie.

A guard announced in Spanish it was time for bed. Juanito and the other boys moved back to their bunk beds, then the lights went out. The room was still dimly lit from the lights in the bathrooms and after a few moments Jamie could see in the gloom.

Sherry took the top bunk bed, while Jamie took the bottom. It was now dark outside the windows, it was nighttime, but they had spent most of the day sleeping and they weren't very tired now.

Jamie laid trying to sleep and thinking about their situation. When he heard some noise, he turned to see the group of boys he'd seen with Juanito earlier sneaking into the girls' section. They led a young girl over to one of the unused bunk beds. They were trying to be quiet, but Jamie could tell they were excited.

One of them stopped to look over at Jamie and Sherry. He whispered something to his friends and they looked over to Jamie and Sherry. Then three of them approached, the other three staying with the other girl, who was now taking off her clothes.

Jamie knew somehow, they were coming for Sherry. They wanted to take her away like they had the other girl and make her take her clothes off. They were bigger than Jamie, but he wasn't going to allow that to happen.

Jamie stood up when they got closer, putting himself between the boys and Sherry and crossing his arms, facing them. They all stood taller than him, but he wasn't going to let them past without a fight. They gestured for Jamie to move and said something in Spanish which he didn't understand; they clearly wanted him out of the way.

Jamie didn't move, clenching his fists at his sides as they got closer.

One tried to push him aside, but Jamie stood his ground. The one closest to him tried again, and Jamie pushed back, then threw a fist at the boy's face. It connected, but it caused a shot of pain up his arm.

"Ouch," Jamie grunted as the boy fell back, bleeding from his lip.

The other two boys advanced quickly on Jamie, then the boy who he had struck got up and joined them. Jamie threw a few more punches, but the other boys blocked them. Someone kicked him in the stomach. A huge fist hammered into the side of his head, making the world spin.

He desperately attempted to throw a few more punches, as well as a few kicks but he was soon knocked to the floor. One of the boys pinned his arms. More kicks came, knocking the breath out of his lungs.

"Oye!" one of the adults called, hearing the commotion.

The boys scattered, heading back to their own beds quickly before the lights came on.

"*Que pasa?*" one asked, coming over to find Jamie bruised and battered, nursing his bloody lip. "What happened here?"

Jamie looked up to see Juanito's friends looking at him from their beds.

He knew better than to rat on them.

"I fell," Jamie lied.

Chapter Four

THE GUARDS DIDN'T BELIEVE him, but they weren't being paid enough to care, apparently. The lights went off again, and they all went to bed. The boys didn't come back, and the girls who had been ushered over to their section of room earlier also went back to their own beds.

Even so, with the pain from the beating, Jamie wasn't able to sleep. Not that he thought he was going to get much anyway.

Eventually, he did manage to doze off for a couple of hours before the lights came back on.

He was tired, but not getting any sleep at night was something that Jamie was getting used to. It wasn't something that he particularly liked, but it was a part of his life that he had been living with for almost two years.

As he quickly made his bed, he noticed that Sherry was still asleep, but he didn't have the heart to wake her. Even so, a couple of the boys approached them.

Jamie straightened up quickly, expecting another fight, but these weren't the same boys who had beat him the night before.

They backed away when they saw him, speaking quickly in Spanish. Or at least, it sounded like Spanish, but he still couldn't understand it.

Finally, one came forward who was a little older than Jamie, with a tougher look to him.

"You don't worry, yes?" he said, his English better than Jamie had heard from their guards. "We are not here to hurt you. Just want to say… good that you stood up to the other boys. They hurt the girls. The guards don't like it, but nobody says who they are, or they hurt you too, right?"

Jamie nodded. He figured that was the case among the children.

"But if you learn how to fight good, push them back, they no hurt you, yes?" the kid continued, offering Jamie a hand. "I can help you fight good. They leave me alone, see?"

Unlike the other children and now himself, Jamie realized that while there were some bruises on the boy's knuckles, he showed none on the rest of his body.

He finally nodded, extending his hand to grip the other boy's.

"I'm Jamie," he said, looking over to Sherry, who was starting to wake up. "And that's Sherry."

"My name is Santiago, but my friends call me Santa," the boy replied with a large smile, showing a missing tooth. "Nice to meet you. After breakfast we practice, okay?"

Chapter Five

SANTA WAS TRUE to his word, and Jamie found himself and Sherry spending more time with the boy. He had learned how to fight and speak English while spending most of his younger years on the streets of Cartagena; learning the language from tourists and fighting to keep others away from his food.

Jamie wasn't sure how the boy had managed on his own and was eager to learn. The fighting methods that Santa used weren't exactly fair, but neither were the methods used by the three boys who had attacked Jamie. They were all bigger and stronger than him, and he needed something of an edge.

Most of the training involved quick hits, since those were what Santa told him would win or lose a fight, and the rest involved moving out of the way. Jamie was quick on his feet, but Santa left him in the dust.

"You need to show pressure," Santa said, and when Jamie showed that he didn't understand, the boy continued. "You fight for life, so act like it. Every punch as hard as you can. Every move as fast as you can. You practice, you get better."

Jamie nodded, somewhat understanding the point.

One morning, a few days later, the men came over to Sherry, who was still in bed, telling her that she was going for a ride with them. Jamie wasn't sure what they had in mind, but the rude gesturing from the other boys was still vivid in his mind.

"If she's going somewhere, I'm going with her," Jamie said, standing up in front of the pair who had come to collect her.

Neither seemed sure about what to do, shaking their heads and talking between themselves. It was clear that neither wanted the trouble, and they quickly turned around, heading out of the room.

When they didn't come back, Jamie assumed that they had decided to not come for her.

***

ONE NIGHT, when the lights went out, Jamie could see Juanito gathering his team again. They didn't look very happy about waking up, but it seemed they were going to try for Sherry and Jamie again.

But this time Jamie was ready for them. Quietly, and as subtly as possible, he wrapped two strips of cloth around his knuckles and pushed himself up as the boys reached their beds. This time four boys came.

They had been expecting the two to be asleep, but seemed undeterred, trying to climb onto Sherry's bed. One had almost reached his target and was fully exposed, so Jamie pounced on him. His fist lashed out with all the power that he could muster, hammering into the boy's stomach.

His breath left him in a rush, and he dropped to the ground with a thud.

The other boys reacted to the threat, but Jamie had taken Santa's advice to heart, immediately bringing his knee up to the groin of a second boy. Like the first, he dropped without a sound.

Juanito was left with just one of his gang, seeming almost unsure of what to do. Jamie took advantage of their hesitation. He grabbed Juanito by the neck and pulled him into the side of the bed, feeling the boy's head hit the wooden structure loudly and hard enough to leave a dent.

The last of Juanito's boys was trying to escape, and Jamie slipped in closer, tripping him up, causing him to land headfirst against another bedframe.

He could hear a noise coming from outside the door as the guards began responding to the commotion. Jamie turned to see Juanito trying to push himself up, looking dazed and slowed.

Jamie noticed a knife glinting in Juanito's hand.

Juanito put up little fight as Jamie yanked it from his numb fingers and tucked it into his own waistband, hiding it under his shirt. He deftly removed his knuckle wraps and hid them under his pillow. The guards turned the lights on and saw Jamie standing over the four boys.

"What happened?" one asked, looking at the four boys all beginning to recover.

"They fell," Jamie asserted confidently, looking down at Juanito. "Isn't that right?"

The boy paused, looking up at Jamie, rubbing his bruised face and nodded. "We fell."

It wasn't an outright lie, Jamie thought as the boys limped back toward their beds. He wondered if they would retaliate with even greater numbers the next time.

Chapter Six

THE STATE OF JUANITO and his gang was clear to everyone when morning dawned, and the happenings of the night before were quickly told and retold among them. Jamie wasn't sure of the reaction to expect from the group.

Afterwards, however, a few of the girls approached him to ask for protection from Juanito's gang, offering cigarettes as payment, but Jamie wasn't quite sure what to make of it.

"Just take them," Santa suggested when they were all in the mess hall for breakfast.

"But I don't smoke," Jamie pointed out. "I don't even like smoking. Where do they even get the cigarettes?"

"They're one of the few things that our guards allow inside," Santa replied. "And we're not allowed to have money. Sometimes the guards even give us smokes to keep us quiet, or if they want one of us to do something. A lot of us end up smoking them anyway, but they can also be used to buy other things, or pay people to do things."

"Do you smoke?" Jamie wondered.

"Sometimes," Santa said.

It seemed silly to turn down cigarettes. Besides, if he was going to be helping them, taking their cigarettes meant that they couldn't smoke them. He wasn't sure if he'd be able to use them for anything, but if he wasn't allowed to have money, at least they were something.

Some of the girls moved over to sleep in the bunk beds beside Jamie and Sherry's. Juanito and his gang didn't bother them for a while, but Jamie had a feeling that this would not be the last that he heard from them.

It was almost two weeks into their stay before the guards again came to take Sherry out on a trip, and this time they agreed to take Jamie along with her. The guards led them down to a car and, once inside, they were both blindfolded.

They drove for what seemed like hours. Despite being blindfolded, Jamie recognized the sounds and smells that only came from a city, and the car kept stopping and starting, which meant at least that they were still in Cartagena. They drove for almost a half hour before pulling into an underground garage, where they were taken into a hotel via the service elevator. If anyone saw them, there was no mention made of the two children being guided to a room on a high floor.

Two men who looked like foreign businessmen were waiting for them in the room. Jamie couldn't be sure where they were from but they spoke Spanish well and they didn't look American. The strangers smiled at Sherry and Jamie, but he couldn't help but feel creeped out by them.

One of the guards remained in the room, keeping an eye on Jamie and Sherry, who were pushed onto a sofa and told to wait as the second business man left the room with the other guards, closing the door behind them.

"Can I get you kids something to drink?" the remaining man asked in a soft voice. "A beer, maybe?"

Jamie shook his head but didn't say anything. He was thirsty but he didn't want anything from this man. He wondered if he would be able to punch his way through this as he had with Juanito's group. He doubted it, but he would have to try if they made to hurt Sherry.

The man shrugged, leaning back in his seat. "It'll help you relax; I'll tell you that much."

Jamie clenched his jaw again, and didn't answer as the door opened again and the other adults returned. The businessman looked angry. He turned to address his partner in a foreign language as the guards pulled the two children from the room and back down to the car.

They probably hadn't come to an agreement on a price, Jamie told Sherry as they were again blindfolded. It was unlikely that the guards cared about what would have been in store for him and Sherry had they been left behind in that hotel room.

He felt sick to his stomach, but he held the feeling in until they were back at what they thought of as home. As soon as they got back upstairs, Jamie found his way to the bathroom and threw up. He told himself it was from riding in the car being blindfolded, but it was probably more to do with the disgust of thinking about what the two strangers had wanted from him and Sherry.

Chapter Seven

IT WAS ONE of those nights where Jamie found his eyes starting to close almost as soon as the lights went off and his head hit the pillow. He hadn't been getting much sleep, worrying about Juanito's gang coming to them in the night, and it was catching up to him. He began to think they might not bother him and Sherry anymore.

He couldn't tell how long he'd been asleep. It could've been a few minutes, or a few hours, there was no telling.

All he knew was that he was instantly awake, looking up into the eyes of Juanito in the darkness of the room. Hands were gripping and pinning his hands above his head. All four were back, and this time they would not be denied.

Two boys were pinning Jamie down, with Juanito holding Jamie's knife to his neck. Two other boys climbed up to the top bunk bed where Sherry lay.

He could hear soft cries of surprise from Sherry muffled likely by the boy's hand, and Jamie could feel a fire in his veins suddenly taking over. He bucked against the grip on his hands and shoulders, fighting to get free.

Juanito paused, pulling the knife from Jamie's throat, showing he had no intention of killing him. It was a moment of weakness, even if the hand was moving up to help contain Jamie, and it was one that he wasn't going to forgive.

Jamie struggled to get his hands free, then he used their distraction to draw attention from his legs, and his knee shot up and hammered Juanito in the temple.

Pain seared across Jamie's arm. He hadn't seen it happen, but he knew instinctively Juanito had cut him. At least it was his arm and not his throat, he thought. Jamie's right hand was free, and his thumb moved up to the eye of the boy closest to him, and he pushed as hard as he could with a loud grunt.

"*Mierda!*" the boy shouted, falling away as Jamie found his arms free again, jerking them away.

One boy remained close to him, looking panicked as Jamie jumped from his bed, screaming and gripping at the boy's throat. Jamie took the boys head in both of his hands and smashed it into the floor as hard as he could. The boy went limp.

Jamie was on his feet again, turning and jumping up to the top bunk as the lights came on. The boys had already torn Sherry's clothes and one of them had climbed on top of her.

Jamie gripped him by the shoulder and rolled them both off of the bed, to land heavily on the floor.

"Stay away from her!" Jamie screamed, recovering quickly despite the pain in his arm. He threw a few hard punches at the boy's head and his stomach before straddling his chest.

Before Jamie could throw anymore punches, he was dragged away from the boy. He managed to kick the boy in the face as he was drug away, leaving the boy limp on the ground.

"Enough *niño,*" shouted the guard pulling Jamie off, and pushing him back onto his bed.

What Juanito's boys had been doing wasn't lost on the men, and Jamie watched from his bed as two boys were dragged from the room, nursing their wounds as Jamie used a knuckle wrap to bandage the cut on his arm.

He saw that Juanito had abandoned the knife on the bed, likely dropping it when he'd been kneed in the head. Jamie kept his eye on the boy who had been ignored by the two guards as he returned to his bed. The boy didn't look up and didn't notice Jamie watching him like a hawk with fire in his eyes as the lights went out again.

Chapter Eight

JAMIE COULDN'T SLEEP, but he was getting used to that. The guards managed to get Sherry fresh clothes, but she clung to his side the whole next day. An indication that the events of the night before was still on her mind. Jamie felt bad that she had been scared, but he was glad that the boys hadn't had the chance to actually hurt her as they had no doubt intended to do.

Jamie needed to do something; just defending himself and Sherry would end badly for him. He had been lucky to get a hit in before anything happened to Sherry this time, but there was no guarantee that he would be able to do that again.

A message needed to be sent. The whole night and day Jamie could feel something hot in his chest and stomach, thinking of the way Juanito had looked down at him in the darkness.

Jamie clenched his jaw as the lights went out again the next night, waiting until he could hear the shallow breathing from the bunk bed above him which told him that Sherry had fallen asleep.

Jamie climbed out of his bed, feeling his heart thudding hard in his chest as he pulled the knife out from under his mattress. He moved over to the bunks occupied by Juanito and his gang, keeping himself low. He wasn't sure what had happened to the boys that had been caught trying to hurt Sherry, but they hadn't been around since then. Now it was just Juanito and one other bad boy.

It wasn't that Jamie felt confident, he just was no longer prepared to be afraid of the bully. He gripped the knife in his hand a little tighter as he moved in next to Juanito's bed, trying to move silently as he approached.

Juanito was sound asleep, but his eyes jerked open as Jamie placed his hand over his mouth. He reached up to resist but stopped when he felt the knife pressed to his neck.

Jamie had vowed to himself that he would kill Juanito. He had pictured it all day and imagined what it would look like when he did.

But as he stood over Juanito, looking at the sheer terror in his eyes, reflected in the meager light of the bunk room, Jamie didn't think he could do it. The boy was a bully, and terrible, but killing him just didn't feel right. Besides, he didn't know if the guards would punish him for killing another boy, and he didn't want to risk being separated from Sherry.

Jamie scowled, pressing the knife a little tighter to Juanito's neck before he pulled away, deciding that he wasn't going to go through with his murderous intent.

But a message still needed to be sent. Jamie looked down to find that the wound on his arm had reopened with the improvised bandage absorbing the blood.

Juanito's eyes looked over to the wound as well, and then to the knife. This gave Jamie an idea. He slowly moved the knife over to the other boy's arm, his terrified eyes watching in the gloom. When he tried to move his arm, Jamie pinned it down with his knee, holding it in place as he dragged the blade across Juanito's bicep in the same way that it had cut Jamie's arm a few nights ago.

The muffled cries were almost inaudible, not waking anyone as Jamie pulled back, leaving the cut as a visible reminder for all the boys of what would happen if any further attempts were made to attack him or Sherry.

Chapter Nine

THERE WERE NO consequences for Juanito's injured arm. Jamie had hoped there wouldn't be, but he was still surprised to be left alone from that point forward, by the guards as well as the other boys. Juanito bandaged his injured arm. The other members of his gang barely even spoke out again.

Jamie knew that wasn't likely to be the end of it, but for now something calming came over him. He was able to sleep a little better, although the many nightmares he couldn't remember often woke him.

The children were separated as usual for showers, and the boys mostly seemed content to leave Jamie alone. Even when he didn't have his knife on him, none of them were willing to come up against him.

It was an odd feeling. Jamie knew for a fact that the others were stronger than he was. Santa seemed just as scared of him as the others were, and Jamie knew that the kid could beat him black and blue if he wanted to.

They all stayed away from him, though, as if they were afraid of him. Jamie wasn't sure if he liked that, but in the end, if it kept them away from Sherry, he would take it.

Jamie finished showering, drying himself off with a towel provided and got back into his clothes as everybody was making their way back to their rooms. Sherry usually tried to find him after the showers, but she was nowhere to be seen.

Jamie asked a few of the other girls if they had seen her but they didn't respond, just looking away from Jamie. He suddenly knew something was wrong. The two guards who usually kept an eye on the group of children were also missing.

Jamie rushed to the bunks and grabbed the knife that he had hidden in his bed, pushing kids out of his way without a second thought. The guards had gotten their hands on Sherry, and he wasn't going to let them get away with that, not if they were taking her for a ride.

Jamie was already running down the steps before he could even think about what he was doing, or what he was going to do when he caught up to them.

As he reached the ground floor, entering a well-lit hallway, Jamie could see two men walking Sherry towards the exit holding her up by her shoulders.

"What is he doing here?" one of the men said in Spanish when he spotted Jamie.

"Leave her alone!" Jamie said, rushing towards them. Two other men stepped into his view, blocking his way to Sherry.

Jamie still didn't know what he was going to do, but he needed to get to the door before they took her out. Hands reached out for his shoulders, and Jamie tried to pull away from them but when they clamped down and stopped him.

Jamie drew upon the skills that Santa had drilled into him. His hand, clenched in a fist, hammered into the groin of the man on the right. The man grunted in pain, doubling over as Jamie's elbow hit the second man's stomach, right where

Santa had taught him to hit. The breath rushed from the man's lungs and he too dropped to the ground.

"Sherry!" Jamie shouted, running after her as the door closed between them. Jamie wrenched open the door and ran out.

A man escorting Sherry turned around, and found Jamie charging at them. They weren't going to let him go with her, not this time. If that were the plan, they would have just pulled them both instead of resorting to trickery.

The man scowled. His fist came up, and Jamie tried to dodge it. He almost did. The punch sailed a little high but clipped him right behind the ear and Jamie hit the ground. The world was spinning, and he could feel his stomach churning.

But he was still awake.

"*Vámonos,*" the man snapped and pulled Sherry toward a car.

Chapter Ten

JAMIE PUSHED HIMSELF up off the ground. The hit hadn't knocked him out, as he thought it would, but the world was still spinning. It got worse when he got to his feet; little flickers of light jumped around in front of his eyes as he struggled to stay on his feet.

But he fought it off. Sherry hadn't gotten too far.

His stomach threatened to hurl again, but Jamie leaned against the door, fighting it back, shaking his head gently; that didn't help. He stopped moving, taking long deep breaths to keep himself awake. It didn't work but did some good when he finally spotted Sherry and ran toward her.

They dragged Sherry, over to one of the parked cars. One of the men walked ahead of the other two, pulling a set of keys from his pocket and pressing a button which caused the car's lights to flash and emitted a tone of three soft chirps. This told Jamie that the alarm was turned off and the car was unlocked.

The man taking the lead opened the back door of the car and proceeded to the driver's seat to start the engine.

Jamie wasn't sure how he was able to run when only seconds before he had struggled to stay on his feet. Putting one foot in front of the other, he began picking up speed. His heart was pounding, and there was a dull ache in the back of his head where he had been punched, but that didn't stop him from running as fast as he could.

He tripped on the uneven ground, but still managed to close in on the men as they pushed Sherry into the car. Sherry fell over onto the seat, possibly asleep.

"No!" Jamie shouted, pulling the knife from his pocket. This caught the attention of the man who had closed the car door on Sherry to turn and see Jamie charging at him.

He had no time to throw a punch this time and Jamie was on him before he could react. Jamie head-butted the man in the stomach, which was enough to double the man over, but Jamie also went sprawling to the ground.

As Jamie recovered and quickly got to his feet, he looked around, suddenly not seeing Sherry. He shook his head to clear it and looked in the car. It hadn't moved yet, but the lights flickered on and then shuddered as the sound of the car's engine echoed in the garage.

"No!" Jamie shouted again. He wasn't sure why he was yelling. His throat was sore and the pounding in his head was getting worse, but Sherry was getting away. The car started fully this time, coughing out a cloud of foul-smelling smoke as Jamie ran toward it.

The world twisted and swam around him, but he reached out for the car door, pulling it open just as it started moving.

Chapter Eleven

THE CAR ACCELERATED toward the exit despite Jamie having the door open. Jamie was barely able to dive into the back seat beside Sherry as the car picked up speed, tires squealing and engine roaring.

Jamie was knocked out of the seat and onto the floor as they hit the ramp out of the garage going too fast. The open door struck one of the pillars, breaking the glass and bending the door frame which caused the door to remain open as they drove out into the street.

Jamie looked around the floor of the car, feeling for the knife that had fallen from his hands. He finally found it and sat back in the seat for a moment trying to catch his breath. The driver was driving madly and didn't pay any attention to Jamie.

"Are you okay," Jamie asked Sherry.

Sherry looked at him with tears in her eyes and nodded. She didn't appear to be physically hurt but she was terrified. Jamie put an arm around her and held her tight.

The car continued moving for a few long minutes until it screeched to a halt again, hammering Jamie against the front seat, and leaving him in an uncomfortable pile on the floor of the back seat.

"No se mueven!" *Don't move!* the man shouted, and Jamie looked up to see a gun pointed at Sherry.

The man cursed softly and pulled a phone from his pocket, the gun faltering so Jamie noticed it now pointed over their heads. He dialed a number and put the phone to his ear.

Someone answered the man's call, and they got to the point quickly. Jamie could hear the excited shouts on the other end of the line. They were talking Spanish, but maybe through desperation, Jamie could understand what they were saying.

"Kill the boy, take the girl to the drop off," he heard the person on the other end say.

They were going to kill him and leave Sherry all alone in this world, without anyone to help her.

That fire in his stomach started up again, his heart thudding and ticking loudly in his chest as Jamie surged off the floor and into the front seat. The man's gun hand was caught on Jamie's shoulder, and he pushed it upwards as the man pulled the trigger.

The sound of the gunshot in his ear deafened him, but he didn't stop. Jamie pushed the knife into the driver's face and was cutting at anything he could find. His ears were ringing, but he sensed the man's screams as the knife cut into his throat, opening it up. Blood spurted out, coating Jamie's arms and neck.

Another shot rang out, but the light faded from the driver's eyes and he dropped back against his seat, body slack and the smoking gun dropping from his lifeless fingers.

Jamie's eyes were tearing up, his ears still ringing as he pulled his knife from the man's neck.

Jamie turned to look at Sherry who had come to and was staring at him with wide eyes.

"Are you okay?" Sherry asked him. Jamie's ears were ringing but he could read the words on her lips.

He nodded slowly. Physically, he was okay, but he had just killed a man. That changed a person. But there wasn't time to worry about that now. He could hear sirens in the distance and knew they had to get away from the car.

Jamie moved down, picking the gun up from where it had fallen on the floor, tucking it and his knife into his pockets before climbing into the back seat.

"Come on, we're getting out of here," Jamie said, tugging Sherry's hand to open the door.

"Oh my God!" she said, her voice slurring as they climbed out of the car. "You're bleeding."

Jamie checked himself quickly. He was hurting and aching, but there was no sign of injury.

"I'm fine," Jamie said. "It's not my blood. Let's go."

They jumped out of the car and ran into the night as the sirens grew louder.

Chapter Twelve

JAMIE AND SHERRY walked through the back streets of the city. They didn't run into too many people, and those they did tried to stay away from them. Jamie didn't blame them; he could imagine how they looked, bruised and covered in blood.

Jamie wasn't sure if that was good or bad, but it sure did simplify matters. Maybe folks in the city of Cartagena were used to the sight of kids covered in blood.

As they walked, the shock wore off and Sherry finally started crying. Not loudly, but rather involuntarily. Jamie would have wrapped his arms around her but figured she wouldn't want the blood on her from his hands, arms, and chest.

Moving through the streets, Jamie finally found a small park that looked to be deserted at this time of day. He saw no hoses or water fountains, but there was a small lake.

Jamie led Sherry over to the water. He could feel the blood becoming sticky on his skin.

They reached the water and without speaking a word to each other, Jamie cleaned Sherry of the blood splatter from the earlier struggle in the car. He hadn't been sure of what to do with the gun, but after a few seconds of tinkering, he managed to remove the cylinder from the revolver.

There were no more bullets, which was a little annoying, but Jamie wasn't sure what he would do with a loaded gun anyway. His ears were still ringing as he crouched by the waterside to wash the blood from his hands.

There was a lot of blood, and it was difficult to get it all off, especially from his clothes. Every time he looked at his hands to check if they were clean, images of the knife plunging into the man's throat flashed through his mind. That reminded him to wash off the knife too. His shirt and shorts were probably stained beyond washing.

"What are we going to do now?" Sherry asked, her voice sounding a little raw as she sat down next to him.

Jamie stared down at his hands, taking slow, deep breaths, trying to calm himself even as he wondered the same.

"I don't know," Jamie finally admitted, hearing police sirens approaching. "We'll figure it out, though."

Chapter Thirteen

JAMIE COULDN'T GET the blood out of his clothes. He stopped trying after an hour of scrubbing. The best he managed was a dull pink that had spread through the fabric.

Jamie dropped to the ground next to Sherry, shaking his head. His ears were still ringing, and he had aches and pains all over. His fingers were aching, but he wasn't sure why, which was also the case with other bruises here and there, but overall, he just felt tired.

"Thanks," Sherry mumbled softly. "For… you know, everything."

Jamie shook his head. "Nothing you wouldn't do for me."

She nodded. "Still though. How old are you?"

Jamie looked up at the odd question. They had been together for over a year now. He just assumed that she knew how old he was, but then he realized that they hadn't actually discussed it. Nor did he know much about her.

"I'm eleven, I think," Jamie said. "I was almost ten when they took me from my school, and it's been more than a year. I'm not sure how long it's been since then, exactly, but I think it's been more than a year."

"They took me when I was walking home from school," Sherry replied, running her fingers through her tangled hair. "I think you're right. It's been more than a year. So, I must be ten now."

Jamie nodded. It was difficult to keep track of the length of time they had been captive. It wasn't as if they had calendars or watches.

"Do you think we'll ever get home?" Sherry asked, looking to Jamie.

He was torn. Jamie could tell that she was looking for comfort, something that would help to keep her spirits up. They had escaped the men holding them captive, but that resulted in no food, no resources and no way to get home that Jamie could think of. He didn't even know how they had come to be here in the first place.

On the one hand, he wanted to say that they were going to get out, find their families and head home now that they were free. But he wasn't sure he believed that anymore. Dan, and Sam were gone. Everyone was gone, except Sherry.

Sam said their parents were killed, but he didn't want to tell Sherry that. He trusted Sam, but something about the story didn't seem right, and he preferred not talking about it with anyone. As long as no one else knew, he could pretend it wasn't true.

"I hope so," Jamie finally said, forcing a smile. "We need to get out of here."

Sherry looked over to where his eyes had suddenly shifted. There were families, mothers with small children, coming into view. Citizens that would likely not take too well to seeing two bloodstained children interrupting their happy afternoon.

"Let's go," she agreed.

Chapter Fourteen

JAMIE WASN'T MUCH GOOD at shoplifting. There was no school or training that could teach him how, but they had no food or water, and they weren't going to survive without it. He wished they'd drank from the lake before they left, but that was no longer an option.

The thought of using the gun to rob a shop for food did occur to him, but if they ever pushed him to use it, he wouldn't be able to. And then he would be arrested for threatening people with a gun.

It was better to just take what he could when people weren't looking, and keep the gun hidden in case he got caught and needed to scare someone with it. That way he could run with what he had without attracting too much attention.

A small convenience store had a refrigerator outside stocked with large bottles of water. Jamie bided his time, waiting for the shop owner to busy himself tending to customers before moving forward, pulling the door open and taking two bottles of water before running away.

He didn't know whether or not the owner had seen him, but nobody shouted or made any trouble as he rounded the corner to join the waiting Sherry.

"Did you get any food?" Sherry asked, but her face fell as all she saw in his hands was the water.

"This was all I could grab," Jamie said, handing her one of the bottles, cool and dripping with condensation.

It wasn't much but it would do for now, as Sherry quickly peeled the top off and took a long drink from the cool bottle of water. It was a hot day; hotter when they were out in the heat, on their own, on their feet and running.

"We have to find a place to spend the night," Jamie said, wiping his face on his sleeve.

"Maybe we can go back to the park?" she asked. "It was nice there."

Jamie shook his head. "I saw police patrolling the area. I think they're there to kick out homeless people. That's what we are now: homeless. We need to find somewhere else."

"Hey, you two!"

Jamie turned around, his hand moving around to the gun that he had hidden in his back pocket.

Two men were standing at the edge of their sidewalk, dressed like tourists. They were speaking between themselves in a language that Jamie didn't understand.

"What... what?" Jamie asked.

"I saw... you steal from the store," one man said, and immediately raised his hands. "I no take you to police. But I buy you and girl some food, and I pay for the water too, okay? Just... I go into the store, and I buy, is that okay?"

Jamie didn't want to trust the man, but the growl in his stomach reminded him that they hadn't eaten all day, not at all since they had run away. Food, no matter the source, was sounded appealing now.

"Okay," Jamie said.

The men walked away and returned a few minutes later with a couple of empanadas, a bag of chips and more water.

"Thank you," Sherry said softly, taking the food from their hands.

The men smiled, speaking more of the language that Jamie couldn't understand, and went on their way. Jamie and Sherry dug in and made short work of the food.

"Wow that was good," Jamie said with a small smile. "Let's find somewhere to sleep now."

Chapter Fifteen

JAMIE JUMPED UP, roused from sleep instantly. His head struck the low roof covering the back of the battered little Toyota pickup truck where they slept.

"Ouch," Jamie whispered, rubbing his head. He turned to see that he'd woken Sherry. The shelter, such as it was, was better than sleeping out in the open, barely.

"What's the matter?" Sherry whispered.

Jamie looked around for the source of the noise that had woken him, then spotted it.

"The people in that house," Jamie said. "They're awake. Maybe they're coming out soon. Come on."

He took her by the hand, guiding her out of the pickup and into one of the alleyways that they had been skulking through.

"I'm still tired," Sherry complained.

Jamie nodded. "Put your head on my shoulder."

They both sat down on the ground, and Sherry leaned into his shoulder, quickly falling asleep again as he wrapped his arm around her. It wasn't the most comfortable way to sleep, but if they were going to get a couple more hours of sleep then they needed to do so before the heat of the day made sleeping outside impossible. He settled into place, letting Sherry settle a bit more as he watched the owners of the house come out and drive away in the yellow pickup truck, leaving a trail of black smoke.

It wasn't long before they needed to move again; more people were moving through the street, and these people, the locals, did not look friendly like the tourists had.

They reached a small outdoor restaurant, where the owners would not allow them entry, but a couple of tourists took pity on them and bought them food to eat. A police car came along and the officer started shouting at them. Jamie gripped Sherry's hand and together they ran off, taking the food that they had been given with them.

"Why didn't we talk to the police?" Sherry asked when they finally stopped, out of breath. "They can help us, right?"

"Right," Jamie said, nodding. "Or they can be like those cops that took money from Sam. You remember the ones that showed up outside the camp when we met. If we run into the wrong one, they might turn us back over to those... people, and since we – I killed that guy, they won't... They'll kill me. And even if we run into one of the honest cops, they might know that we were involved in killing that guy. That means prison, or maybe worse."

She nodded, tears running down her cheeks. "You know we can't run forever, right? We won't be able to get back home on our own!"

Jamie scowled. "I know!"

"What's your plan?" she shouted at him. "Do you have a plan to get us home? You don't, do you?"

Jamie clenched his jaw, trying to keep the threatening tears from falling from his eyes as Sherry turned around and stormed out of the alleyway.

Chapter Sixteen

SHERRY WAS ANGRY so Jamie gave her some space. They had both been through enough together as it was, and maybe she just needed a moment or two to gather herself before coming back.

Jamie still followed her as she started wandering the streets, running away for a few blocks before slowing down to a walk. Jamie kept his distance, but still kept her in sight. He still felt responsible for keeping her safe, even if she had apparently lost her faith in his ability to do so.

If he was being honest with himself, Jamie had abandoned all hope of getting back home, and therefore had no plan aside from surviving as long as possible. Maybe her parents would still be looking for her, and someone would recognize her and send her home. But for him it was different; he'd been gone for much longer.

It was likely that people back home thought he was dead.

Jamie shook his head at the thought, moving forward as Sherry approached what looked like a bus stop, just as a bus was arriving. A large group of people disembarked, including vendors with their produce, slung over their backs from a stick. These were all locals, though, since most of the tourists tended to use taxis.

"Damn it," Jamie growled, losing sight of Sherry in the crowd. His heart started pounding a little harder as he picked up his pace, looking around the group. If he saw her, he would be able to pick her out instantly, but there were so many adults around him that it was impossible to see through the group.

They moved quickly, mostly ignoring Jamie as a street urchin. A few of the older women clutched their purses and belongings a little closer, expecting that he might try to pick their pockets, but Jamie passed them by without so much as a glance.

She was no longer on the street. Had she seen him following her and taken advantage of the distraction to run away?

No, that didn't seem like her.

Jamie moved quickly, retracing his steps, feeling the panic starting to well up in his chest until he found a small one-way street that they usually used to hide in.

She was sitting on the sidewalk, face in her hands, and sobbing.

Jamie moved in and sat down next to her, not saying a word. He didn't know what to say to help, and all he could really do was be there with her.

"I'm sorry," she finally said, her voice cracking as she gripped his hand again. "It's... I'm hungry, and thirsty, and tired. I don't know how... I..."

"It's okay," Jamie mumbled, hugging her and letting her sob into his shirt. He could feel her tears through the fabric, but he didn't really mind.

He was only happy that he hadn't lost her.

The faint rumble of thunder had his eyes turn upwards towards the sky where he could see the clouds starting to darken above them.

"I think we better get moving," he said, patting the top of Sherry's head. "I don't think we want to get caught out in a rainstorm like this."

Chapter Seventeen

THE STREETS GREW even more hectic when the rain started coming down, and it wasn't long before they were both splashed with mud and soaked through. Getting off the streets seemed to be a priority, and they found a park in the city where Jamie could see a small gazebo at the top of a hill.

Sherry and Jamie both moved inside. Despite the warm weather, the rain was still cold enough to chill them to the bone, and they stayed inside for a while to warm up. It was hot enough inside that the cold quickly passed.

It wasn't long, however, before Jamie saw a few local kids about their age playing in the rain in their underwear. They ran up to the top of the, dragging big pieces of cardboard behind them. Once at the top, one would climb on and slide all the way down the hill. Some younger kids joined them, stripping off their clothes and sliding down the hill on their bottoms. Sometimes the other kids would make a wrong turn and the sled would turn over, but then the children would continue sliding or rolling down the hill on their own, laughing as they did.

For a moment, Jamie couldn't help a small wish to be one of those kids instead of living on the street. He didn't like the feeling, and quickly pushed it to the back of his mind. Sherry was standing at the window, watching them.

"Do you want to go out there to play with them?" he asked.

She shrugged her shoulders. "I don't know. Could be fun, I guess."

"We'll get wet," Jamie pointed out.

"We're already wet, and it looks like they're having fun," Sherry insisted. "Come on, don't you want to go out and have some fun?"

Some fun? An odd concept, so long absent from his life. The thought made an odd smile come to his face.

"Sure, why not?" he finally replied.

"Yes," she hissed, running out of the gazebo, and rushing out into the rain that they had been avoiding only fifteen minutes ago. Jamie smiled as Sherry talked one of the girls into letting her use the makeshift sled. The other children pushed her over the hill and she slid all the way down, skidding across the puddles that were starting to form at the bottom.

Jamie couldn't help a small smile as he ran down to help her bring the sled up.

"Do you want a turn?" Sherry asked.

"No, you go again," Jamie said with a laugh, this time helping the children push her. "You keep going until you tip over, that's the rule."

She was halfway down when the sled overturned, throwing her head over heels the rest of the way down. Jamie's worry over her being hurt quickly fell away as she pushed back up to her feet, laughing and pulling the sled back up the hill.

It was nice to see her laughing again. Jamie didn't think he would ever see that again.

He hoped it would last.

Chapter Eighteen

THEY WERE STILL HOMELESS in a foreign country, but Jamie tried to forget about that as they played. One of the other boys gestured for Jamie to take off his shirt and hang it with the clothes the local kids and hung over a fence at the bottom of the hill. He obliged and when realized how good the rain felt against his bare skin, he took off his shorts too.

Once the rain stopped, the children all had somewhere to go, probably inside to dry off and warm up. Sherry and Jamie, who had been having fun until that point, were saddened by the reminder that they didn't have anywhere to go. They began wandering again and eventually made their way to a small abandoned warehouse where they hung their clothes up to dry and Jamie laid down to rest on some old canvas bags.

"That was fun," Sherry said as she straightened their clothes on the improvised line. "Been a while since…"

She didn't need to say it aloud, and Jamie nodded in agreement. It had been a while, but he wasn't going to keep dwelling on it. The warehouse that they'd picked was abandoned for the moment but there were people working nearby.

Sherry didn't seem worried about that, however. The sun came out from behind the clouds and shone down on them bright and warm. Sherry laid down next to Jamie and yawned. They hadn't slept much the night before and it wasn't long before they both fell asleep.

***

IT COULD HAVE BEEN hours or minutes that passed, but the sound of shouting around them got Jamie on to his feet quickly. A group of men were yelling, seemingly having arrived at work to find Sherry and Jamie in their way.

At least their clothes were dry; they got dressed quickly, running out of the door that one of the men was holding open for them.

"They seemed nice enough," Sherry noted in passing when they came to a halt.

"They were yelling at us to leave."

"Sure, but they could have been a lot meaner about it. They just wanted to get back to work, I think."

Jamie shrugged his shoulders. It was nice that Sherry was still able to think about the needs and wants of others. He found that all he could be worried about was what was happening to them.

"Let's go," Jamie said, nudging her shoulder gently as a large group of tourists came into view all heading into town, taking pictures. This was their chance.

The tourists were the most giving and generous, with the fewest questions. Locals tended to be a little thriftier, suspecting children wandering around their town as pickpockets and thieves. There wasn't much that they could say to change their minds.

Jamie smiled as a couple of notes and coins were pressed into their hands. Sherry was having better luck. She looked younger, and the fact that she was a girl made them feel a little better about giving her money. Jamie didn't mind, knowing that she would share the money with him anyway.

"Hey, you two, where are you from?" one of the men asked in a strange accent.

Sherry answered before Jamie could. "I'm from Canada, he's from the US. We were kidnapped and brought down here, and we're trying to get back home."

The man laughed. Jamie narrowed his eyes, seeing that they didn't believe her. They considered it to be either a joke or just another sob story to get more money. The rest of the tourists moved away quickly.

"Why don't they believe us?" Sherry asked.

Jamie shrugged. "I don't know. Maybe they just don't want to. At least we have some money for food tonight."

Chapter Nineteen

"WE NEED TO get out of here," Jamie said.

Sherry looked around, turning from the meal that they had just purchased from a street vendor. They were getting used to the spicy food common in this country by now, but it still left Jamie sweating.

"What?" she asked. "I'm not finished yet."

Jamie pointed towards one of the nearby hotels. He could see a security man walking over to a police car that had just pulled up. He was talking to the officers and pointing to Sherry and him. Jamie noticed then that the other beggars usually in the area had all vanished. They knew better than to deal with the cops.

"Maybe they can help us?" Sherry insisted, finishing her food and tossing the wrappers.

"I don't think so," Jamie said. "Come on, we need to…"

He froze as he saw another car pull up, cutting off their escape. Two officers quickly walked up to Jamie and Sherry, placing a hand on their shoulders, keeping them in place.

They spoke in Spanish, asking what the two children were doing there.

"We were kidnapped," Sherry insisted in English. "They took us from our homes and brought us here. Why can't you just help us to contact our parents?"

The officers either didn't understand or didn't believe them. Jamie kept as compliant as possible, giving Sherry's hand one last squeeze before they were pushed into the police car. The officers didn't look happy about having the dirty children in their back seat, but they said no more as they started the car.

"Do you think they're taking us to the police station?" Sherry whispered.

Jamie clenched his teeth, trying his best to keep a positive mindset. "I heard them say something about taking us back where we belong."

"I guess… that's not the police station then?"

He shook his head. "I don't think so."

Sure enough, he saw no sign of a station in the area. They were heading into one of the slums of the city which as they slowed down, appeared the kind of place where they would not be causing any trouble.

It didn't look safe, but then again, neither had any of the places they'd been. Jamie could only guess that these people were going to do a lot more than yell and call the police. They needed to be more careful now.

The officers pulled them out of the car roughly and without another word, slammed their doors and drove off. The message was clear: stay out of the nice part of town.

Jamie didn't know what else they could do, but he wasn't going to push them. At least they hadn't bothered to search him. He still had the empty gun, his knife and a little money left over after buying their lunch.

"Why won't anyone help us?" Sherry asked, and Jamie saw that she was trying not to cry.

"They will," Jamie assured her, helping her back to her feet. "Eventually. Someone's got to."

He wasn't sure if he believed that, but it was a nice thought.

Chapter Twenty

THERE WERE A LOT more people on the streets in this area, but none of them were tourists. A lot of them were children, dirty and dressed in rags, or in the case of some of the younger children, not dressed at all. Adults wandered the streets or sat in abandoned buildings.

Not knowing what else to do, Jamie and Sherry walked toward a bus station where they saw some local kids outside begging. When they got closer, they saw they weren't just begging, though. Some were also pickpocketing. Jamie watched as one child shouted, attracting the attention of people passing by as their friends moved in behind grabbing whatever they could from pockets and purses. It reminded Jamie of Oliver Twist, only most times the children didn't get anything, and they often had to run away when people caught them trying to pick their pockets.

There were shacks put up with makeshift materials, mostly pieces of wood and aluminum, with chunks of rock and concrete put in here or there. Wiring from inside the buildings provided lit up a few scattered light bulbs which flickered.

Jamie had never seen such a place. People who were all in the same boat as him and Sherry or worse off. He gripped her hand, keeping their meager belongings close, as they moved through the groups.

One of the children saw Jamie and Sherry sticking together, and approached them cautiously, speaking Spanish. He was about Jamie's age and he had long, unruly dark hair. He was filthy and he wore only a tattered pair of shorts and sandals made from plastic bottles. He carried a plastic bag with more bottles and cans in it.

"What's he saying?" Sherry whispered.

"He's asking if we have somewhere to sleep," Jamie said, and turned to the boy. "Non," he said, and shook his head.

The child indicated for them to follow him. The sun was setting so Jamie and Sherry followed the boy through the streets towards a section where he could see a group of children starting to settle in for the night.

"Seems like the kids around here stick together," Jamie noted as they joined the ad hoc little town of homeless children.

"That's nice," Sherry said, yawning. What seemed to be social workers came around to them, serving disposable bowls of soup and slices of cheap white bread to the children. Sherry and Jamie tried to explain where they were from again, but from the awkward smiles of the women dressed like nuns, he could see that they didn't understand what was being said.

"Just our luck, I guess," Jamie grumbled.

"We have food," Sherry said softly, turning to look up at Jamie. "We have a place to sleep."

"Probably want to keep a hand and an eye on what we do have."

Sherry smiled and leaned against his shoulder. Jamie could hear her breathing starting to slow and deepen. Even with the nap that they'd had earlier in the day, it had been a long day with not enough sleep.

Jamie looked around at the homeless people and was once again reminded that him and Sherry were also homeless. These people all had about as much as they did or less, but there was something wholesome about how they were willing to share what little they had with two strangers.

If nothing else, it showed that while the rich in the city disliked having poor people around, those that had less were more willing to show their more human side.

The sky darkened as the sun dropped out of sight. The nuns were handing out blankets, and Jamie claimed one for himself and Sherry as they settled in for the night. Thankfully, the heat of the day didn't dissipate quickly in the humidity, so it wasn't cold at all, which allowed Jamie to lean back against one of the shacks, and drift off to sleep.

Chapter Twenty-One

MORNING CAME ALONG quickly, and Jamie found himself actually feeling more rested than he'd felt in a while. Almost impossibly, he thought.

The rest of the children were up with the sun and a quick nudge from them had Jamie and Sherry up off the ground too. The nuns weren't coming back to collect the blankets, so Sherry, who looked a little more tired than usual, kept the one they had wrapped around her shoulders, as they followed the group of children heading towards the streets.

Some looked like they were going right to work, but the one that had directed Jamie and Sherry indicated for them to follow him. Jamie was fairly suspicious of the child's goodwill, but as a larger group of about a dozen children joined them, he relaxed a little.

Besides, with his knife and the gun, he could probably scare people long enough to run away if things got ugly.

They came to a halt outside of what looked and smelled like a restaurant, or maybe a bakery. The children sat down and waited as if this was a normal routine and so Jamie indicated for Sherry to do the same.

After about fifteen minutes of waiting, the nearby door opened, and a thick set man walked out carrying a couple of black trash bags. Instead of tossing them into the trash bins, he left them at the foot of the steps.

The children approached the bags, opening them to expose a treasure of bread and pastries. The flour dusting suggested that the bread was probably stale and old, likely having not been sold over the past few days. However, it was still food, and better than what he could probably expect to buy with what little cash they still had.

Jamie picked out a couple of smaller loaves and one of the pastries stuffed with mango jam, and handed them to Sherry, who quickly wolfed them down. She spilled a little of the jam on the ground but didn't appear to mind. Jamie grabbed up a couple of pastries and began eating too.

"See?" Sherry asked, wiping the crumbs from her mouth and smiling. "Things could definitely be worse. When was the last time you remember getting two square meals one after the other?"

Not since they had left their captors, but Jamie didn't want to say that out loud. They still needed to find some way to get food and shelter, and he only wanted them to worry about one thing at a time.

They didn't want to return to the tourist area, but the transportation areas in the slums were picked dry. A couple of the larger children, and a couple of grownups along with them shouted for Jamie and Sherry not to intrude on their territory. While others made sure that neither were going to be able to sleep in some abandoned shacks that they found, forcing Jamie and Sherry back to the spot that they had spent the night before. The nuns were back, giving out soup and bread and blankets.

And once again, they were set to spend the night under the stars, with Sherry curled up beside him, mumbling softly in her sleep.

Jamie couldn't help a small smile. They didn't quite have a full belly, but at least they weren't starving. It wasn't a permanent solution for them, of course, but it would do for now.

One problem at a time.

Chapter Twenty-Two

IT WAS MORE of the same the next day.

Jamie and Sherry ended up finding their way to a bigger bus stations where fewer gangs were at work, with more police presence, but they still didn't have much success. Having to get around quicker to avoid the cops getting a lead on them didn't allow much time to beg properly. The tourists had been a little more giving at least, without having to be asked; they just saw children in need and handed out change.

The locals that passed by pretended not to see them; pretending to be in a hurry to get to or from work, and likely not wanting to end up in some kind of pick-pocketing scheme.

By the time lunchtime rolled around, they were both hungry and they shelled out the last of their cash to buy a meal from a street vendor. As he had promised himself, Jamie made sure that Sherry got the larger portion of the food.

"What do you think we should do next?" she asked, settling into a seat, eating slowly.

Jamie shrugged his shoulders. "Begging isn't going to get us much. I was thinking we could ask those nuns if they need someone to work with or for them, but I don't think they'll be able to understand me if I ask them. I mean, I don't see the harm in it."

He looked up, seeing one of the local gangs coming in closer. By now, they knew better than to get into any kind of dispute with those they came across. They were likely armed and connected with the local authorities, or at least, more connected than Jamie and Sherry were.

"I guess we could always try to work out a way to start pick-pocketing like the other kids," Jamie noted once they were safely away from the bullies. "Like you could make a scene for them, and I grab the money, and we run away."

"I don't... want to," Sherry said softly, shaking her head. "Don't want to steal."

"We may not have a choice. The bread place had less food than before, and there were more kids. Who knows how long those nuns are going to keep coming around, and in the meantime, we have no money and no way to get any? We need to find something."

Sherry nodded, sighing softly. "We'll figure something out. We have so far, right?"

She wasn't wrong, of course. They had been pushing their luck ever since they'd run away from the captors, and there was no telling how long that was going to last, but it wasn't as if there was an abundance of choices. They were going to need to rely on their wits a bit more over the next few days if they wanted to survive.

For the moment, though, it was another stay with the group of children outside. Jamie found that it was a little more difficult to sleep than it had been before.

Chapter Twenty-Three

NO MONEY, NO FOOD and no prospects. The bakery was closed for the day, by the looks of it, and there was no chance that they were going to find another place from which to get food. A couple of the local restaurants were open, but since it was Sunday, most of the people were at church. Even the owners of the restaurants, and the workers didn't want to give away free food without permission.

Jamie was starting to feel desperate. Sherry looked more tired than usual, and as the day started to get hotter, she was looking more and more sluggish as the seconds ticked by.

"I'm just hungry, that's all," she explained, shaking her head. Lunchtime came around, and still no food. He supposed that living on the street meant that they were going to have to get used to being hungry from time to time, but that realization wasn't going to make it any easier.

Around midday, when the sun was scorching, people began to leave church, going out for a meal at the local restaurants. Among the many people, most scowled and shouted in passing at the two in Spanish. Jamie couldn't understand what they were saying, but from the context, at least, it didn't sound good.

Suddenly, it looked like they were onto something. Sherry followed a restaurant worker out back behind a building, to find him discarding food. Some of it at least still smelled good, or maybe they were just too hungry to care. Still, Sherry pulled a bin over, to discover takeout boxes filled with rice, some even contained meat and vegetables.

"Better than nothing," Sherry said, choosing one that looked like it hadn't been touched. She ate it right there by the dumpster. Jamie was hungry too, and found himself taking a couple of bites, but once that edge of hunger was gone, the food started smelling a little off to him and he discarded what was left.

"Are you sure this food is okay?" Jamie asked. "It smells bad."

Sherry sniffed at her box. "Smells okay to me," she said.

He wasn't sure if he would be able to tell if the food was bad, though, and so as Sherry continued eating, he didn't stop her. They were no longer in a situation to be picky about what they ate.

Once they were finished, Sherry started to look better, acting a little more like herself as the day went on. They still didn't have much luck making money, and as they made their way back to the spot in which they had been spending the nights, Sherry was starting to look a little pale in the face.

"My stomach hurts," she complained, clutching at it. A second later she turned around and threw up on the sidewalk.

A couple of nearby strollers quickly backed away, cursing as they crossed the street. Jamie scowled at them, shaking his head as he helped Sherry straighten up.

"How do you feel?" he asked. She only managed to shake her head while clutching at her stomach.

They reached the spot again, but Sherry shivered and moaned softly, still looking like she was going to be sick. Jamie pressed his hand to her forehead but she didn't have a fever, which was odd. He remembered Sam shivering like this too when he was feeling sick, but he always had a fever when that happened.

One of the nuns approached them slowly, questioning them in Spanish. It was clear what she meant.

"Ella... enferma," *she's sick.* Jamie replied in halting Spanish. He made a gesture of eating, and then pointed at his stomach.

That was succinct enough, and the nun called one of the other nuns and told her about their situation.

"Vamos a la clínica," *go to the clinic* the other lady said helping Sherry on to her feet again.

"Where are we going?" Sherry asked, sounding sluggish.

"To get some help," Jamie replied, squeezing her hand again. "I hope."

Chapter Twenty-Four

THE ORPHANAGE WAS for girls only. Jamie wasn't sure how a rule like that was even instituted. He knew a thing or two about how religious orders worked, but if a boy got sick, would they just not help him?

It didn't really matter though. He wasn't sick, and Sherry was getting help. There wasn't much else that he could ask for except maybe a place to sit while he waited.

As it was, he was stuck outside, sitting on the sidewalk, waiting for news about Sherry. All he could be happy about was that they had at least gotten her some help.

The sound of the door opening behind him had Jamie jumping to his feet as a couple of young women walked out. They definitely didn't look like locals. One had blonde hair, while the other had brown curly hair, but they lacked the skin tone of the locals.

"Hey kid, is this your friend?" they asked, speaking very slowly, like he wasn't going to understand.

Was he starting to look like a local? He had been around long enough.

"They won't let me in to see her," Jamie said, trying to keep the tears from rolling down his cheeks.

"Yeah, they have some... rules in there," the blonde woman said. "Wait, your English is very good. You're not from around here, are you?"

Jamie looked around, feeling the twisted knot in his stomach return. "I... well, I'm from Massachusetts. My name is Jamie. My friend in there is Sherry, and she's from Canada. English Colombia or something."

"You mean British Colombia, right?" one of the women asked, and both exchanged a quick glance. "How did you end up here?"

Jamie clenched his teeth, feeling a couple of hot tears run down his cheeks despite his best effort. "I was..." his voice clamped up for a minute, not sure if they would believe the story, but he had to try. "We were kidnapped. It was a long time ago. We got away from the bad guys, but even the cops won't help us. Please, is Sherry okay?"

The two women exchanged another look, and the blonde woman stepped forward, lowering herself to eye level with him. Then she looked at her friend. "I remember all those kids getting kidnapped a while ago. Must have been over a year ago, actually. Do you think..."

"If he's telling the truth, that means that he and Sherry have been missing all that time."

If he was telling the truth? Jamie felt his cheeks flush. "I am telling the truth! Please, is Sherry going to be okay?"

"Hey, hey, now, it's okay, kiddo," the brunette said, putting her hand on his shoulder.

"I don't have money," Jamie said quickly. "But I have..." he pulled out his knife and the gun he'd fought off of the driver. "I got these off of the... well, the knife I got from the place where they were holding us. I stole the gun from the guy that drove Sherry away."

Both girls backed away at the sight of him bearing arms, and Jamie quickly realized his mistake, laying both on the ground. "Please, I don't have anything else to pay you with. Just make her feel better. There's no bullets in the gun."

They gingerly picked both up off the ground, trying to make out whether Jamie was actually trustworthy or not. He wondered if they dealt with this kind of thing often.

"Okay, I'm calling this in," the blonde nurse said, quickly turning to head back into the building.

She took both weapons with her. Jamie thought that meant that they were accepting his payment.

The brunette stayed with him. "Look... Jamie, right? We're going to be looking into getting you back with your parents, and Sherry too. In the meantime, we're going to be taking Sherry to a proper clinic to see a doctor, and you can come with us. Would you like that?"

Jamie could only manage a slow nod. He thought again about how Sam had said his parents weren't dead. Was he about to find out if it was true?

Chapter Twenty-Five

THIS WAS THE FIFTH SOLDIER to come into the room at the embassy and ask him the same series of questions. What was his name? What were his parents' names? How long had it been since he'd gotten to Colombia, and how had he arrived there? Where had he been kept this whole time? Jamie always gave them the same answers, which were correct, as far as he could recall. The submarine trip, staying with Carlos and Sam, the moving around, the house where the girls were taken out for rides.

He even told them about stabbing the man with the knife, but when he was asked if they were going to throw him in jail for it, they laughed, said no, and ended the interview.

He felt guilty for being annoyed with them. They had given him fresh clothes, and food as well as a bed to sleep in, which was also appreciated. They even let him see Sherry while she was recovering, letting them eat together and play old video games on the TV in her room.

This was as good as life had been for him since he had gotten here, but they were just asking him the same thing over and again and they never answered any of Jamie's questions.

He wondered if they couldn't just film him saying it all the one time, and that would be it. Jamie wasn't about to complain, though.

The men in fatigues finally told him and Sherry that their parents hadn't been killed by the mafia, in contrast to what they had been told, but were in fact on their way to fetch them. Jamie wasn't sure how to feel about that. Sherry was obviously very excited by the news, bouncing up and down in her hospital bed.

It was difficult. He had been gone for long enough for none of it to seem real. He knew he should be happy, but he was scared. It had been two years since he'd been kidnapped.

News that both their parents would be arriving in a few hours hit Jamie like a ton of bricks, and he didn't want to leave Sherry's side when they arrived. His parents looked exhausted. His dad had lost a great deal of weight, and his mother looked as if she hadn't slept in weeks. And they were all over him.

The touching, the hugging, the crying just felt odd somehow. Sherry and her parents looked so happy. Jamie wasn't sure what to make of that, but he forced a smile even though he could feel that his cheeks were wet from crying. They kept asking if he was okay, and Jamie didn't know what to say.

"We're going home, baby," Sharon said as she wrapped Jamie in her arms. "I've missed you so very, very much!"

Jamie could feel his chest convulsing as sobs pushed their way out. What was he going to do now? They wanted him to stay with them. And while he wanted that too, there was just something inside him saying that it wasn't right. Something was off about it but he couldn't tell what.

All he could do was clutch at his parents, hold them close, and hope they didn't notice.

Chapter Twenty-Six

JAMIE COULDN'T SLEEP. He had thought that was going to be a thing of the past. For all his exhaustion over the past two years, it was annoying to realize that now that it was all finished, he still couldn't sleep.

They were moved out of the embassy, and with Sherry on the mend, they were prepping both families to return to their respective homes; Jamie back to Boston, and Sherry back to Canada. Sherry's parents hadn't even let him say good-bye before whisking her away. Now they were all in a hotel near the airport, waiting for a flight that would take them all home and end this seemingly never-ending nightmare.

But there he was, just staring up at the ceiling. It wasn't that his mind was too busy to fall asleep, or like he had been trying to think up ways to avoid it.

But here, in bed, hearing his parents snoring quietly in their double bed and having one of his own just didn't feel right, somehow.

Jamie pushed himself up, carefully peeling the sheets off before walking over to the bathroom, silently closing the door and turning on the lights.

An odd sight, really. Jamie wasn't sure how someone could look in the mirror and feel alienated by the face looking back, but there was no denying that. He was thinner than before, but there was a lean musculature showing too. His cheeks were gaunt, and his eyes deep with a sort of redness and desperation. Having to fend for himself for two whole years was etched across his face as if one of his classmates had drawn it on with a magic marker.

Classmates. He was going home now, and probably going back to school, maybe play some kind of sport to pass the time, or maybe his parents would want him to play a musical instrument instead. Maybe sign up for some advanced placement classes.

He couldn't explain it, but after all this time away, the very concept just felt so foreign.

What were all of his friends going to think? Oh, wait, no, they would have all graduated, heading off to middle school or something. He would be stuck catching up with them because of his time spent here. Learning the kinds of skills that would help him survive here but would be useless back home.

Home?

It just didn't fit. He couldn't say why but thinking of his time back home just felt like someone else's memories and life that he was returning to.

Jamie looked back up into the mirror, and realized the stranger there was crying again, which he had been doing a lot of the past few days. He shook his head, moving away from the mirror and turned the bathroom light off. That was better.

He slipped out again, standing over his parents' bed. Practically strangers, really, and he knew that he was a stranger to them now too, despite all their talk of love and missing him. They even said that they had been looking for him all this time, which he believed.

It wasn't a conscious decision, but Jamie found himself picking up the bag that they'd packed for him and walking over to the door. He remembered the door number of Sherry's room too. He would see if she wanted to come with him.

He doubted she would because she was happy to be back with her family. She probably didn't see a stranger in the mirror like he did. She was a good girl and deserving of everything good in life.

"What the hell am I doing?" Jamie whispered to himself but couldn't stop putting one foot in front of the other until he was in front of her door, about to knock.

The lock clicked, and it opened. Sherry was standing in the frame, dressed in frilly pink pajamas.

"Hey," Jamie said softly.

"Hey back," she replied.

Chapter Twenty-Seven

SHARON GROANED SOFTLY, rising from the bed. She was used to being awake around this time; worrying about being in a foreign country ever since they'd arrived in Colombia, as well as worrying about her son. Jamie had made for a lot of sleepless nights, trying to find some new way to track her baby down whenever they lost his trail.

This was one of the first times that she could remember that she had managed to get some real sleep, but her body clock was still telling her that it was time to get up.

She grumbled and went to the bathroom, intending to go back to bed when she saw that Jamie's bed was empty.

The horror that filled her had her frozen for a few seconds, trying to convince herself that she was seeing things.

But no, the bed was empty. She ran over to Harry, shaking him awake.

"What… what?" he mumbled, still half-asleep, looking around and trying to put his glasses on.

"Jamie's gone," Sharon said loudly, shaking him again.

"He's been... wait, what?" Harry asked, waking up fully, and looking over to Jamie's bed. Sure enough, a second pair of eyes revealed what she already knew had happened. Harry climbed out of bed, and put on his clothes and they searched the room once more, just to make sure that Jamie wasn't just under a bed or on the balcony.

But he was gone.

Harry and Sharon left the room, and made their way to Sherry's parents' room. They were still asleep when Harry started pounding on their door, but sure enough, Sherry was gone as well.

"Do you think they went off together?" the father asked as they dressed and joined Sharon and Harry on their search.

"They've been together for months," Sharon pointed out. "I don't think that they would just leave each other alone after so long together. I think they would have gone together. The question is... where?"

They moved out to the lobby, where the night receptionists had not seen either of the children. The pair of parents were about to call the police for what felt like the millionth time when a bellboy on duty said that he'd seen two gringo children heading out to the playground outside the hotel.

Sharon, Harry and Sherry's parents quickly rushed out the back door into the dark playground, where they could see two dark figures. Sherry was on the swing, swaying gently and Jamie was sitting at the edge of the jungle gym.

They stopped talking immediately at the sight of the adults coming into the playground.

"Oh my God, Jamie!" Sharon shouted as she rushed over to wrap Jamie up in her arms. "Don't you know how worried we were? You can't just go wandering around again!"

Jamie said nothing in response. She supposed that he had been wandering around on his own, or with Sherry, for God knows how long, so there was no point in really telling him how unsafe it was to go out on his own.

He probably already knew the dangers better than she did.

Chapter Twenty-Eight

A GROUP OF PEOPLE was waiting for them at the airport when they arrived back. His family, sure, with both sets of grandparents, all his aunts and uncles, as well as a wide selection of others. Some were his friends, together with their families, as well as people that had heard about what had happened, and wanted to welcome him back. A couple of his old teachers had made up the welcome committee too.

There were even a couple of reporters with cameras, smiling and asking about how it felt to be back home. Jamie didn't know how to answer that. Would they understand if he explained that all he felt was confused?

Probably not.

His parents were quick to intervene, saying that he was still recovering and was in no shape to answer any questions, quickly moving him to the waiting car. Nobody really wanted to know about what happened to the other children who had been kidnapped. Some had been recovered, sure, but a lot of them were still missing.

Nobody remembered them. Maybe they'd forgotten about Jamie too, and were only reminded when he was finally brought back.

It didn't really matter. Jamie was quickly pushed into a car, where his grandparents were hugging him and asking how he felt. A small party had been arranged once they got back to the house, that Jamie had almost forgotten about.

His mother's parents were talking about how they knew a doctor that was good with children who could examine him. One of his aunts talked about how she knew a child therapist that Jamie could talk to, but all Harry and Sharon could say was that they were just happy to have their baby boy back.

It was weird, though; he didn't feel back. People were talking to him, but also practically ignored him. They were talking about him, but never once wanted to dig deeper into what had happened to him, or the other children. It was like they didn't even want to know.

Everyone was talking about how it was just the happy ending that they had been hoping and praying for. If that was the case, why didn't Jamie feel like it was happy, or the end?

They didn't get him back to school immediately, of course. An extensive medical checkup had a doctor telling his parents that he was marginally malnourished and showing signs of injuries which hadn't healed properly, as well as scars that Jamie had almost forgotten about.

Otherwise, he was as physically healthy as any other boy his age. The psychologist said that mentally was another matter, but Jamie could hear the man tell his parents that he was clammed up, refusing to talk about what had happened while he was missing.

Of course, he wasn't going to talk to them. They didn't even want to know about it, right? About how he missed Sam and Sherry. People didn't want to know that. All they wanted was for him to put on a smile and say that he was getting better. That was the happy ending that they wanted to hear.

He pulled out his phone and dialed the number that his parents had given him. Sherry didn't have a phone of her own, but her house did.

"Hello?" answered a woman's voice.

"Hi," Jamie said softly, clearing his throat and then speaking again. "This is Jamie. Can I talk with Sherry, please?"

There was a pause as Jamie sensed that the woman – Sherry's mother – didn't want to think about the situation anymore either, and that Jamie calling to talk with her daughter wasn't helping.

"Sure," the woman said with a soft, fake chuckle. "I'll get her, just a moment."

A few seconds passed, and Jamie could hear the woman's muffled voice, asking if Sherry wanted to talk to Jamie.

Another pause.

"Jamie?"

It was Sherry's voice. She sounded healthy at least, like she was getting better after her sickness.

"Hey... hey, Sherry," Jamie said, feeling his voice crack. "Are you okay? How's it going in Canada?"

"I don't know," she replied, honestly.

"Yeah. I feel the same way."

They didn't speak for a few seconds. It was nice to just know that she was there, even if all he could hear was her breathing. He missed her, he realized. Weird.

"How about you? You sound tired."

Jamie blinked. "I... I haven't been sleeping."

"Why not?"

"Because..."

He didn't know what to say. Nightmares were something that he'd been dealing with since the kidnapping, but they hadn't stopped him from sleeping before.

"I just don't feel right," he said, finally.

"I know the feeling." Sherry agreed. "I keep thinking about the other children that we left behind. My mom says that a few of the kidnapped kids were recovered, but a lot weren't. I thought after we got back and told the cops what we knew, they would find the other children, but I feel like they've given up. How can they just give up?"

Her voice was cracking and she was tearing up, and all Jamie wanted to do was reach out and grab her hand, and squeeze it like he had so many times while they were together on the streets.

"I miss you," she whispered softly.

"Yeah... I miss you, too," Jamie said, trying not to cry. He was failing, and a couple of hot tears ran down his cheek.

He brushed them away quickly. "Look, I've got to go, it's late. I'll talk to you soon, okay?"

"Okay, call me tomorrow," she said. She sounded so sad that Jamie longed to be there to comfort her.

The line cut off, and Jamie put the cordless phone down on his desk. He then sat for a long moment staring at it, deep in thought. Finally, his mom tapped softly on his bedroom door and told him it was time for bed. Jamie opened the door, handed her the telephone, and went to brush his teeth.

Epilogue

JAMIE RETURNED TO SCHOOL, and it was good to be back home where he no longer feared for his safety on a daily basis. The stories about his captivity, escape and having to fend for himself, together with the scars to prove it all, made him popular amongst his peers, but he didn't feel like he belonged anymore. His classmates still acted like little children, while Jamie, who had spent over a year away, felt more like an adult now. He didn't care about any of the stupid concerns of other 12-year-olds and he couldn't talk to them about what was really on his mind.

Jamie couldn't talk to his parents either; he had tried, and they were willing to listen, but they didn't know what to say. His mother had mentioned that a counselor might be able to help, but Jamie didn't think so. The only person he could talk to who really understood, was Sherry. They sometimes talked about what they had been through together and what would have happened had they not escaped. But they mostly spoke about what the other kidnapped children were still going through and what people could do about it.

Harry and Sharon were supportive of this, but they thought he was too young for a cell phone. They did give Jamie a phone card so that he could call

Sherry any time without too much expense. They even promised to take Jamie to Vancouver to visit Sherry in the summer.

When Jamie wasn't busy talking to Sherry or doing his homework, he spent most of his time reading about kidnapping and human trafficking. He was appalled to learn that thousands of children, mostly girls, were victims of human trafficking in the United States every year. When he looked at worldwide statistics, the number climbed into the millions. He and Sherry often spoke about this and while she didn't share his obsession for research, she agreed that something needed to be done, and they vowed that one day they would make a difference.

Dear Reader,

I hope you enjoyed reading the story as much as I enjoyed writing it! As a token of gratitude, I've included a free sample of my most popular book. I'd also like to invite you to sign up for my mailing list. You'll get a FREE copy Escaped (a novella) and I'll let you know when I publish a new book or when I have a special deal.

Thanks for reading,

JJW jjwestauthor@gmail.com

Keep reading for a free sample of:

Twelve Days of Trauma

Get your FREE book!

Click, tap or type in bookHip.com/lkcwpk

Keep reading for a free sample of:

Twelve Days of Trauma

Twelve Days of Trauma (sample)

Chapter One

December 13th

I DON'T KNOW what woke me up, but my heart was racing. It could have been a bad dream. I looked around the dark room, and then I squinted at the time on my phone. It was 5:42. I closed my eyes and tried to remember what my dream was about but I came up with nothing.

I turned on the lamp and saw that Suzy was still asleep. No surprise there. Even if I had screamed out loud, she might have slept through it. I could only see the top half of her face and her messy, light brown hair above the blanket.

The small smile that touched my lips quickly disappeared. Something was bothering me, nagging at the back of my brain, and I couldn't figure out what it was. It hadn't been there when I'd gone to bed, but now it wouldn't go away.

I had learned from my years as a cop to trust my instincts; they had saved my life more than once. Those years were behind me now but the cop's instincts were ingrained into me. A bad feeling in my gut often meant something terrible was going to happen and this one felt like the real thing. Or maybe it was nothing.

I sighed, looking at the time again. 5:48. My alarm would go off at six o'clock. Might as well get up. I unlocked the screen and was about to open the email application but then I hesitated.

I turned to Suzy again and decided to watch her wake up instead. Seeing her grumble and groan about having to get up in the morning always put a smile on my face. I thought that might lift the cloud of gloom that had been hanging over me.

She'd gotten fast over the years, and the alarm clock barely had time to beep three times before Suzy, eyes still closed, slammed her hand down hard on the clock, bringing an end to the annoying sound.

She groaned, scowled, and shook her head as she pushed herself up from the bed, shoving the covers off. Her messy hair completed the image of a bear waking from hibernation. I smiled at the thought.

"What are you looking at?" she growled (she actually growled). I couldn't stop the laughter from erupting. She threw a pillow at me and lay back down, stretching her body.

"Nothing," I replied in between gales of laughter. "Nothing at all." I used the top sheet to wipe tears from my face.

She grinned too so I moved over to her side of the bed and put an arm around her. "One more day," she said. "Tomorrow, we can leave Celia in your folks' care and take a break. I can't remember the last time we slept in."

"It's been eighty-four years," I said, my voice sounding old and cracked.

She laughed as we started making the bed. We went through our routine that we'd polished to perfection over the years, and twenty minutes later we both left the bedroom freshly showered and ready for the day. Suzy headed for Celia's bedroom to wake her up while I headed downstairs to get breakfast started.

I got out the eggs, bread, butter, milk, and, after hesitating a moment, grabbed a small piece of remaining cheddar that probably wouldn't keep while we were away. There was still tightness in my stomach as I started grating the cheese and stared out the window over the kitchen sink, wondering again what could go wrong today.

"Ouch!" I said, looking down at my finger as blood began to drip on the plate among the shredded cheese. I forgot about the feeling of impending doom for a moment while I went to the bathroom to tend to my injury.

Ten minutes later, Celia came bursting into the room, as was her custom. Her straight blonde hair was already in pigtails which bounced with every step. Her big blue eyes tracked me and she came to stand by my side on her tiptoes, trying to see what I was doing.

"It smells good, Daddy! What are you making?" she asked excitedly. The girl could eat.

"This is just toast with butter," I said, holding up a slice for her to see. "You probably smell the cheese omelet. Watch out though, there's a little bit of Daddy somewhere inside." I held up my bandaged finger.

"Uh-oh, Daddy got a 'boo-boo'," Suzy said as she walked in and headed straight for the coffee maker.

It felt comfortable and relaxing, almost, as we ate together. Then the girls got bundled up and headed for school.

"Oh, I almost forgot, the van is making that noise," Suzy said as they were almost out of the door. "So, I'll take the car to work?"

I nodded. "It's like a rattle, you said?"

"Yeah, when I hit the brakes," she said. She paused for a moment, looking at me. "What's wrong?" she asked, her expression one of concern.

"Nothing. I Just remembered something about work," It was a lie; my feeling of impending doom had returned and she'd seen it in my face. "I'll get the van sorted out. Remember, it's Friday today." I winked at her. We hadn't told Celia we'd be picking her up early from school today and heading upstate to my parents' place.

"I love you, Tim," Suzy said. She returned my wink but she didn't smile. She hadn't bought my lie. "Say bye to Daddy, sweetie."

"Bye, Daddy!" Celia shouted. She was always shouting these days. "We're doing presents at school today!"

"I hope you get something good! Love you girls. Have a great day!" I called as they closed the door behind them.

The bad feeling was back with a vengeance as they walked out the door.

Chapter Two

IT HAD FALLEN TO THE BACK OF MY MIND while the girls were getting ready, but once they were gone and I had the house to myself, there it was again. Like my gut was trying to tell me something but didn't know how.

It was getting to the point where I couldn't focus on anything else. I had a list of things to do before we left town, and only a couple of hours to get everything done. That feeling kept nagging at me and distracting me.

On top of everything, I had to get the van checked out for the rattling noise. "That must be what's bothering me," I said out loud. "The van's making a funny noise. Once I get that fixed there will be nothing to worry about. Then I can stop talking to myself like a crazy person."

I closed my laptop and slipped it into a backpack, and then I grabbed a jacket. I was out the door, in the van and on the way to the shop within minutes.

It was the top-rated garage covered by our insurance. They already knew me and both of our cars well. The shop was fully decked out for Christmas with garland in the windows, Jingle Bells playing, and Christmas tree shaped cookies next to the coffee maker in the waiting area.

"Tim! What can I do for you today?" the head mechanic, Jackson, asked with a pleasant smile. He was a large, muscular man with dark skin and he had a Santa Claus hat on his bald head. He already had a work order in hand, ready to fill it out.

"Well, the wife told me that she heard the car making some weird noises yesterday," I explained. "I didn't hear anything on the way over, but since we're heading upstate to visit my folks, I told her I'd get you to have a look."

"Better safe than sorry, right?" Jackson said with a laugh. "Give us a little while and we'll check it out. What kind of noise?"

I described the noise Suzy had mentioned and he went out to get the van. I snagged a Christmas cookie, opened my laptop and settled in to one of the uncomfortable fake leather chairs. Twenty minutes later, the van drove past the window and into the street. Probably one of the mechanics taking it for a drive to listen for that sound.

A little while meant a couple of hours, apparently. It was a good thing that I brought my laptop with me. I got a few of the most important things ticked off on my to-do list. The first year had been tough, but I had managed to earn a decent living doing accounting and online advertising for small business owners who were usually too busy or lacked the skills to do it themselves. It wasn't as exciting as being a cop, but I set my own hours and I mostly worked from home except for occasional meetings with new clients. Suzy was happy that I was home every night and she didn't have to worry about me getting shot at work.

"I'll tell you something, Tim, we can't hear any noise either," Jackson said once they were finished. "We did a full inspection and greased your ball joints in case they were making noise. Engine, drivetrain and everything are in good shape. Could have just been a pebble in a hubcap or something. Your tires and your rear brake lines are a bit worn though. I recommend new brake lines and we've got some snow tires on sale if you like."

"I'll take the tires and the brake lines," I said with a small, forced smile, looking at my watch. It was almost eleven. "Better safe than sorry, right?"

Jackson sensed my impatience. "Alright. It's already on the lift so we'll have you on the road in twenty minutes."

Chapter Three

MOST GARAGES in my experience liked to slow their work down so they could charge more for labor. Jackson's crew were the exception. They had a reputation to maintain, and it wasn't long before I was on my way back home with a new set of winter tires and new brake lines. All worth it for peace of mind, right?

Then I heard it on the way home. It was like a rattling in the back. It wasn't distinctive, and at first, I thought that it was just my imagination. But my imagination wasn't making the windows shudder as I pulled into the driveway. Something was wrong.

"I'm not going crazy," I whispered to myself, almost in a chiding voice as I pulled the van into our garage, waiting for the door to close before I stepped out and walked around the van, looking for something wrong. I stopped at the left rear wheel, where I could see that the lug nuts hadn't been tightened. The short drive had rattled a couple of them loose.

That was unacceptable. They needed to be better than that. I took a picture but held back on calling Jackson to give him a piece of my mind. I was already behind on what I needed to get done. Best to just focus on that for now. Get ready for the drive upstate. Dream about being able to sleep in for the first time in forever.

I grabbed my own wrench and tightened the nuts myself, double-checking the other wheels as well. Then I sent Suzy a message saying the van was all good and I headed back to my office to get some work done.

It was still difficult to focus, but it was a little easier to shrug the unsettling nagging in the back of my head off. At least the car was in tip-top shape. Or so I thought.

Chapter Four

I GOT THE BAGS IN THE VAN AND CHECKED MY WATCH, expecting Suzy to show up any minute. My phone chirped with a message.

It was from Suzy. "Not done yet. Can you grab Celia first, then pick me up at work?"

I sent her a thumb up and sighed. Suzy was a dental hygienist and she only worked while Celia was in school. She'd only booked a few morning sessions today but sometimes patients showed up late or things took longer than expected. Usually not a big deal but today I wanted to hit the road without any delays.

I parked in front of Celia's school as the first snowflakes started to fall. I looked up at the sky. Thick cloud cover meant more would be on its way soon. So much for beating the storm.

The classroom windows in view outside were decorated with paper snowflakes, the kind kids had been making since I was in school. "White Christmas," the classic version I liked, was playing softly in the administration office.

"Hi," I said the secretary. "I'm here for Celia Jacobs. I called yesterday about fetching her early today."

"Sure, just one moment," she said thumbing through some papers. "Here we are, just sign here please." I signed where she indicated. "Okay, just have a seat and wait for Celia here."

"Thanks," I said with a smile, sitting in a seat that was much like those at the repair shop. Five minutes later, a teacher brought Celia in.

"Daddy!" she said, coming for a hug. "Why am I going home early?"

I thanked her teacher and we headed out to the car. The snow was already falling heavier.

"We're headed to Grandma and Grandpa's house early," I told her. "There's a big snowstorm coming so we'll try to get there before that." Fat chance of that happening, I thought, looking up at the sky again.

Celia literally jumped up and down with excitement. My folks spoiled her rotten whenever we went up to visit, and so I could understand her excitement.

"Can we make a snowman?" she asked. "Where's Mommy?"

"She's just finishing up at work, so we'll pick her up there," I said. "And I don't know about a snowman but I'm going to make some snowballs!" I gave her a mischievous smile and she giggled.

I strapped her into her seat, sent Suzy a text that we were on the way, and we made the short drive to Suzy's office. "Let it Snow" was playing on the radio as the flakes swirled around outside. "XFM weather, including what might be a record-breaking snowstorm, coming up next!" the announcer said.

Suzy was waiting outside when we got to the dental clinic. At least we didn't have to wait for her, I thought.

"Mommy!" Celia said as Suzy climbed in. "There are presents in the back!"

"I know, sweetie, and most of them are for you!" Suzy said, reaching back to tickle her. "Did they find the cause of that noise I heard?" She asked as she put her seatbelt on.

"They did a full inspection and they couldn't find anything," I replied. "I let them sell me some new snow tires and brake lines through. Just to be safe."

"Thanks, babe, you're the best," Suzy said with a small smile.

"The car will be okay here for two weeks?" I asked.

"Yep, Dr. Anderson let me have his reserved spot in the underground," she said. "He's driving to Jersey so he won't need it."

The plan had been to stop at Celia's favorite burger joint on the way out of town or get some lunch we could eat on the road, but the snow was falling hard now. A diner seemed like the better choice to get a bite to eat and wait for the snow to slow down a bit.

I wasn't very hungry so I just ordered a salad. Suzy order the soup and a sandwich. We let Celia have her favorite, chicken nuggets (which she always called McNuggets) but with mashed potatoes instead of fries. The food came quickly and we ate and listened to Celia chattering excitedly about all the fun things we'd be doing at her grandparents' house.

I looked out the window as we finished, noting the snow hadn't slowed down. If anything, it was snowing harder than before. Celia didn't mind, bouncing in our booth as Christmas music played in the background and flakes swirled around outside.

"I think we need to call your parents, Tim," Suzy said, leaning back in her seat and taking a long sip from her coffee. "Let them know that we're going to be late."

"Good idea," I said. I dialed them on speaker and put my phone on the table.

"Tim is that you?" my mother said.

"Hi Mom, it's all of us," I said.

"Merry Christmas, Grandma! Merry Christmas' Grandpa!" Celia shouted, getting the attention of the rest of the diner's patrons for a second.

"Merry Christmas, pumpkin!" my mother said, laughing.

"We might be a little late in getting there," I said. "Snowstorm is picking up."

"No worries about that, baby," she replied. "You just drive safe now, you hear?"

"I'm not your baby," I grumbled under my breath.

"You'll always be my baby," she insisted. "Love you."

I sighed before replying. "Love you too, Mom."

We paid the bill and headed for the car. I helped Celia into her booster seat, then bent to look at the wheel nuts I had tightened earlier.

"Something wrong?" Suzy asked, noticing me scrutinizing the wheel.

"One of the nuts was loose when I got back from Jackson's, but I tightened it," I said. It was actually all five of the nuts on one wheel. "I'm sure it's fine now."

Suzy heard the rattling first as we merged onto the highway. "There it is again," she said. "The same sound it was making yesterday."

I turned off the music (another Christmas song) and listened. Even Celia was silent, sensing our fear. I didn't hear it at first, then I touched the brakes and it was there, faintly. It sounded different from the sound of the loose wheel earlier. It only seemed to happen when I slowed down.

"Probably another loose nut," I said, pulling over into the breakdown lane. The sound grew louder as I pushed harder on the brake pedal to bring the car to a stop. "I'll check."

I looked at the wheel again and the nuts appeared to still be tight. I opened the hatch, moved the suitcases and Christmas presents and got the emergency lug wrench.

"Is it okay, Daddy?" Celia asked. Her little face was frightened, tears threatening to pop out of her eyes.

"It's fine Cee-Cee," I said. I'm just going to double check all the wheels.

I put the lug wrench on the first nut and, with a grunt, managed to tighten it a bit more. The others on that wheel were the same. I then went around to all of the other wheels and checked them all, but they were so tight I couldn't even get them to budge. Celia and Suzy watched worriedly out the windows while I worked amidst the swirling flakes.

"All set now," I said with more confidence than I felt, as I got back in the driver's seat. "To Grandma's house, we go!" I turned up the radio to ensure we wouldn't hear the rattling sound and Suzy sang along with "Jingle Bells."

Chapter Five

"I'm hungry!" Celia whined from the back seat, five hours later.

"I know, baby, we're almost there," Suzy lied, leaning over to the space between the front seats to look at our daughter. "Why don't you watch another movie? You liked that one with the snowman, remember?"

The truth was, we were only halfway there. Traffic had slowed to a crawl as lanes needed to regulate clearing by tractors, forcing the people taking the highway into single lanes as they navigated the slippery, tricky streets. The going was steady, but much too slow.

"Can I have another cookie?" Celia asked, tilting her head.

"In a little bit, pumpkin. Just watch the movie, okay?"

Ordinarily, we would have just let Celia recline in her seat for a nap, but she had just graduated to a booster seat, held in by her seatbelt. Since then, she didn't fall asleep in the car very often.

"I'm hungry!" she declared less than five minutes later. "And I need to go to the bathroom."

Turning around and snapping at her wasn't going to do anything. Besides, I needed a break from driving too. My hands were aching from gripping the steering wheel, and I wouldn't mind stretching my legs.

"Cee-Cee baby, there's a stop a few minutes away," I said, squinting at signs. "Think you can hold it until then?"

"I think so," she replied, pouting her lips.

I smiled up at her through the rearview mirror before returning my eyes to the car in front of me. Heading forward at twenty miles per hour was better than a traffic jam, but only just. It was a little more stressful too since I needed to keep an eye on what was happening in front of me in case a sudden stop was needed.

We pulled off the highway as the signs around us told us that we had arrived in Binghamton. The truck stop had the look of a place that catered to more than just the occasional trucker. As we pulled into the parking lot, the sight of Christmas lights set up inside was all the welcome we needed.

The snow was thick on the ground so I carried Celia through the worst of it, then she didn't want me to put her down until we were inside. Her and Suzy headed off toward the restrooms while I found us a booth.

"Hi there," a waitress said, handing me a menu. She was probably in her late forties but not unattractive with long dark hair, brown eyes and a bright smile. "Heck of a storm out there. Coffee?"

"Yeah, we needed a break," I said, returning the smile. "Two coffees please."

"Sure thing," she said, filling two cups and putting a handful of cream and sugar on the table along with another menu. "The special is meatloaf. I'll be back in a moment to take your order."

The restaurant had a comfortable, homey feel to it. There were a few wreaths around and a real Christmas tree. Soft music played in the background. I felt the stress of the drive draining from me as I sipped my coffee and scanned the menu. Celia and Suzy joined me.

"Special is meatloaf but I want a cheeseburger," I said. I wasn't hungry but Suzy would know something was wrong if I ordered another salad.

I headed for the bathroom myself. As I stood at the urinal the bad feeling returned. Why was it so persistent?

"We ordered," Suzy said when I got back.

I sat down and before I could speak the server came with two plates of meatloaf, potatoes and vegetables. "There you are," she said. "I'll be right back with the burger. More coffee?"

"Yes please," I said and I set to work cutting Celia's food while she refilled my cup and Suzy dug in.

"How are you all liking your food?" the waitress asked twenty minutes later.

"Daddy didn't finish his 'booger'!" Celia said and giggled. She was in a much better mood with some food in her belly.

"And she had all my fries," I said, grinning and kissing her gently on the top of her head.

"Where are you three headed tonight?" the waitress asked.

"Well, we were on our way to Syracuse," Suzy answered. "But with this weather and this traffic, I don't think we'll make it tonight."

"Yeah, you're better off finding somewhere to spend the night and getting a fresh start in the morning, especially for the little one's sake," the waitress said.

"I'm not little, I'm seven!" Celia declared, holding up the correct number of fingers.

"Can you recommend a hotel?" I asked.

She gave Celia a high-five. "I've got a few I can recommend," the waitress said with a laugh. "But with a storm like this they fill up quickly. How fussy are you?"

"Not at all," I said, glancing at Suzy who nodded. "A hot shower and a clean bed will do."

"I know a place that always has rooms," she said. On the back of an order bill she wrote "Big Bing Inn" and handed it to me. "You've got GPS?"

Chapter Six

BINGHAMTON, AS IT TURNED OUT, WASN'T THAT LARGE OF A CITY. The roads were a lot less-travelled in the city than the highways were. We headed toward the Big Bing Inn and, as the server had predicted, we passed several other hotels with "No Vacancy" signs along the way.

"How are all of these places full?" Suzy asked, keeping her voice down as Celia was dozing in the back. "I mean, seriously, what's the attraction in Birmingham?"

"Binghamton," I corrected her as I struggled to keep the van on the two-lane road. Those snow tires were turning out to be a good investment but the rattling sound had returned. "Pretty sure most of the folks are just heading somewhere else, babe," I said, flinching a bit as what felt like the twentieth four-wheel-drive pickup rushed past us at a speed that could only be described as dangerous. "These are the places that are closest to the highway so of course they are full. We've got inside info from our friendly server, so we don't have to waste any more time."

Suzy smiled, leaning back in her seat and staring at me. "How is it that you're always so calm all the time?"

I shrugged. "I work from home. Less stress means that I can help you carry some of your load, as it were."

She opened her mouth to say something just as another pickup rushed past us, splashing a wave of slush onto the side windows. "Geez, can't these people slow down?"

"Maybe they're just testing out their new snow tires too," I said under my breath. The same thing had been annoying me, of course, irking that bad feeling that had been plaguing me since the morning. People going too fast on slushy and snowy roads would only end in disaster.

"Or maybe they're in a rush to get to the nightclub next to the Big Bing," Suzy said.

"Better heading to the club at that speed than away from it," I pointed out.

"I guess that's a good point," Suzy grumbled, shrugging her shoulders. "Let's just hope that the snow is keeping all the parties indoors, so the noise-look out!"

I looked forward just in time to see a row of four or five bright lights, much too high to be headlights, headed straight for us. I pushed on the brake pedal and the van slid in the slush. The bright lights were headed for us. Suzy screamed. It all happened in slow motion, but I somehow knew the lights were going too fast to stop. I let out a scream of my own. Then everything went black. The last thing I remember was the sound of breaking glass and twisting metal.

See Twelve Days of Trauma in store

More by JJ West

USA: bit.ly/JasperWestBooks

INTERNATIONAL: bit.ly/JasperWestWorld

Get your FREE book!

Click, tap or type in bookHip.com/lkcwpk

Printed in Great Britain
by Amazon